Powers
&
Dominations

Powers & Dominations

A NOVEL BY

Robert Early

Houghton Mifflin Company Boston

1975

FIRST PRINTING   W

Library of Congress Cataloging in Publication Data

Early, Robert.
  Powers & dominations.

  I. Title.
PZ4.E13222Po [PS3555.A694]   813'.5'4   74–20575
ISBN 0–395–20285–X

Printed in the United States of America

This book is dedicated to the five who have most helped with it: Anne and Robert Lyons, Elizabeth McKee, Dorothy de Santillana, and Jonathan Galassi.

No, I would not
do it: hang there
by nails—

tho our quick age
has neater ways
of death—

for now, sitting
here in a green
April,

how could I go
from loveliness
to that?

Or how could I
presume that my
blood sings

whatever dark note
it is that makes
a god?

—FRED ECKMAN

Powers
&
Dominations

ONE   GILES LOGAN, new abbot of Boldface Abbey, left Morning Prayers annoyed that only four of his monks had showed up, and knowing that this kind of absence was lately routine. The Abbey was old and the monks thought they were secure; they had long ago abandoned all but the bare essentials of the monastic observance in order to devote full time to Boldface Institute, the small men's college they ran.

They said it was impossible to do all the work of administering and teaching and still be absolutely faithful to the Divine Office. Some had women friends, some drank, almost all watched too much television. They did this much against Giles's orders, too, though he was helpless to do anything about it. He worried about his job. What was an abbot to do when half his community didn't obey him?

He went up directly from the chapel to his room on the second floor of the monastery, where he put his head down on the desk. Even now he was still trying to flesh out the creases that were left in his face from sleeping there. Then he made a memo:

FROM THE OFFICE OF THE ABBOT
CONCERNING: tardiness at the Divine Office
Where was everybody on the 12th?

He wouldn't post it, of course, but he let himself grow a little more comfortable thinking it was the right thing to do. The abbot folded his hands in his lap, resisting the impulse to fart. He thought he might save it until later, and he worried that someone passing in the hall would hear, but then he couldn't hold back.

Next he sorted the morning mail, pleased that the top envelope had a familiar letterhead. And inside had the expected note from Vinnie Dano saying that he would be down that weekend. It was on a 6 x 10 piece of Vinnie's own prescription paper. Giles smiled as usual, thinking it fortunate that Vinnie lived only 180 miles away in Atlanta and had his medical practice there. Vinnie was the only one Giles felt comfortable talking to these days, what with the way things were going. They were old friends, and Giles imagined himself comfortably saying to Vinnie, "My monks really do care for me. They do, you see, because I've done everything for them."

Trusting Vinnie, he could also have said, "Damn them all!"

But that wasn't the point exactly because Giles had said these things often, and it was becoming old that Vinnie came down on weekends and listened to him complain. This morning there was something new. It wasn't only that Boldface Abbey was coming apart or that Giles was blaming himself for it; there was a strange new light pursuing him of late. He accepted the slants of midmorning daylight as though they should not have been there. He felt ironically deprived of appropriate solitude.

He leaned back at the desk and collected a neat pile of memos before him. He shuffled them. His hands were thumping the pages. The memos read OPERATING SUGGESTIONS, and the abbot really didn't look past the first few lines of the twelve or so sheets of paper scrawled in familiar handwritings. He knew what the memos said. The top one, in the hand of the monastery archivist, Father Affirmo Biggsbee, said: We are out of Aqua Velva in the commissary. The Abbot knew this, and he knew that the second memo complained of a broken toilet.

Giles glanced again at Vinnie's note. He could see, between words, the top of his own head in the mirror on the far wall of his adjoining bedroom. His closely cropped hair seemed washed on, and he stood up, driven to deal with the further unpleasantness of his appearance. He was going to examine a few new ways of wearing his pectoral cross when he heard the knock at the door.

What now?

Father Brendan Price was there. He was nearly drunk, as he often was. He was not too drunk to think himself undignified, and so he was grinning flamboyantly. The abbot realized he had forgotten sending for the priest.

"You wanted to see me . . ."

". . . but I think it would be better to say what I have to say when you're . . ."

"You afraid to say the word 'sober'?"

". . . well, Father, you are . . . intoxicated . . ."

"You mean 'drunk'?"

Giles thought of the priest as an old friend also. Brendan was once his confessor, and was like a lot of older monks who had seen their students advance to the top of the monastic hierarchy. The thing was that Giles used to allow the

3

older man the kinds of follies he was accustomed to. For a lot of reasons it was different now. And there was the other thing as well.

"Father Brendan, what about you and Myrtis Crawford? You and Myrtis Crawford again!"

Brendan mocked him, falsetto. "What about you and Myrtis Crawford again!"

He sat down unpenitently and twisted his hands in his scapular. He expected this. He was smarter than Giles and his only reserve was in thinking his former penitent a bungler. It was common enough for monks to be amused at thinking themselves able to threaten the world to which abbots owed an exclusive fealty, where human souls were in the balance.

Brendan said, "It's really none of your business."

"But the disgrace," Giles said.

"Ah Myrtis, Myrtis," Brendan said, pretending reflection. He stared at the wall, though his face finally had the edges of an apology coming up. At fifty-five he was youthful. He was a type that they all had studied at one time or another in the histories of monasticism. The old word was *gyrovague,* a monk who roams. That was the oldest problem possible, and Brendan had, in Giles's view, dealt with it in the most predictable way. He and Myrtis Crawford had been together for twenty-five years, since the war, since she came to work at Boldface Institute as Brendan's secretary. He used to be Dean of Students, and he first gave her perfume and jewelry and candy as if he were a soldier.

The story was well known, and Brendan admitted freely that he took those things from the collections that were made for the Red Cross. He earlier told the abbot that he had been

4

remorseful all along. But he said, "I've watched Myrtis getting old with me." Her fine round face had shed its softness as the war dissolved, the excitement of finding new hiding places turned to dependency. Anybody could see. It was good that they finally didn't care who knew about them.

The monastic community knew. At this point Brendan hadn't even tried to blame it on anything. He never had thought of leaving the priesthood either. It just went on, and he considered himself and his Myrtis above everybody's censure.

Nobody thought him callous nor ugly. Giles didn't. His condition didn't, at the moment, distress Giles, though he knew the priest wanted to be thought of as a renegade. It was the perfect example of what was wrong with Boldface Abbey. He was teasing Giles. It was an inevitable fact that all monks sooner or later got to know the entrapments of their way of life and then the ways out. Giles and Brendan had talked about this before.

"But thank God for Myrtis," Brendan said. He looked sheepishly at the abbot. He measured the moment against what the old friendship led him to believe was on Giles's mind.

"You know," he said, "we've done it, ha, ha, in the loft, ha, ha, and in the basement, ha, ha, and in the . . ."

Giles could only say, "My God, Father."

He couldn't look at Father Brendan without wanting to smile. It hadn't been long ago that they regularly talked about Myrtis in a different way. And they talked about the problems of this life. Giles wasn't the abbot then, and it was especially clear that Giles felt this at the base of his agitation: before he became abbot, of course Myrtis hadn't mattered.

Before that, he had trusted Brendan's notion that he and Myrtis had what they all longed for and what they needed. Brendan thought monks all too gaunt and neurotic. Believing in the conventions had never helped, and so it was a simple matter that Brendan's look recalled the recent past when he and Giles and the rest of them had got tired of the way Boldface Abbey was being run.

It was the leadership, to begin with; in this case the inept Abbot Wilfrid Coogan, who was abbot for over fifteen years and had got laughably tired of it. He made no rules that worked, and Giles and Brendan and the others complained at the lack of community spirit. The old abbot collected photography equipment and made movies in the basement. He said, "I'm busy with my hobbies. I'm entitled to these hobbies. What's all this about community? Leave it to God!"

It had infuriated Giles and Brendan to remember that in earlier years Wilfrid had been a complete tyrant. His first serious prelatial act was the confiscation of electric fans. "I don't care what you say of this being the so-called twentieth century. I don't care if it's so-called hot in Georgia, either. Monks are supposed to be content with the meanest and worst of things."

He argued that the perfect monastery, for instance, was the one in which monks prayed all day. Then he took away the cards and newspapers. He gave them paddles to tuck in their shirts. When he saw a monk taking up anything more than confessional time with a woman, he sent him off to be a military chaplain.

This was the tradition against which Giles rose at a chapter meeting and told the old abbot, "Frankly, you aren't

6

really much of a leader, and I hate to say it, but either shit or get off the pot!"

Giles remembered how the old abbot had smiled the smile of the relieved, how he had embraced Giles when he relinquished the pectoral cross.

Also remembering, Giles watched Brendan's unsuspicious face forgive the intrusion into his privacy. The older monk's eyes bolted in the passing history of Giles's own bungling, eyes which were saying that Giles had followed exactly in Wilfrid's tracks.

It was true.

"We accept the burden," Giles had said, and the editorial *we* was his first mistake. He told the monks that some of them were lazy and misguided. He said, "And it's still true that we have a Holy Rule."

Father Affirmo Biggsbee, leading the instant opposition, cried, "Is this a travesty, or what is this? The Holy Rule is antiquated as everybody knows."

There was the purpose, and at the heart of it were these situations irksome beyond endurance. This was what kept Giles at his desk. It was where his feelings came from.

He looked at the OPERATING SUGGESTIONS, remembering that he had put them out in the hope that his monks would use them to advise him of spiritual problems. Some of them said he ought to resign immediately. They complained of the cigarette supply, of the length of the Divine Office, of no variety in the selection of shaving lotion. Affirmo flippantly demanded colored undershorts.

Now Giles *had* to be looking at Father Brendan Price with complete abandon. He wasn't angry. He wiped away the sweat from his forehead, resisting another impulse to fart.

7

He wanted to fart with Father Brendan there. He wanted the priest to hear him.

"We'll go on with this another time."

He turned his back, but Brendan stayed in his chair. There was a quietness, an agitation in the quietness which then stoked Giles's regret; the old man was superbly silent. Giles didn't like hurting him.

Brendan said, "Well, there is a God, you know. That's the last thing we can count on." He said it knowing the abbot's mind, and still wanting to tease him. He didn't apologize about Myrtis, but he finally did say that he was sorry for being sentimental, for leaving only with an aphorism.

"You try too hard."

So that when Brendan left, Giles went and slammed up the room's only window. He listened to the midmorning sounds again, and watched the sun dangling above the water tank on the eastern side of the property. He was aware of this without knowing why, and he was preoccupied especially with the sun.

The chapel was below, and the garden. He ignored all but the summer colors, which he squinted to see like a painter. The shape of the buildings, an H, was for Hegel. Alcuin Hegel, the founder, who had been solely responsible for the Victorian designs and the indestructible qualities that were quaint in their decay. This abbot had thought Boldface Abbey would endure, and, as history said it, he charged that he would see to its future himself. He had whimsically named it Boldface for this reason. He emerged as its first abbot in 1908, wearing the robes of a self-made prince. He possessed the same kingdom of ornate buildings, a throne of cedar, two pectoral crosses set in gold, a now-lost ring of office with his motto: *Carpe diem.*

Giles translated as Father Affirmo Biggsbee would have: Carp every day.

He surveyed the buildings as if they did belong to another age, somehow amused. There was a remoteness even though the sounds he heard were of morning traffic from the nearby town of Boldface, of the whistles from the cotton mills. Here was the travesty — it was Giles's kingdom too.

Ring, ring, ringringring.

"Adelaide Hone," said the voice, and Abbot Giles put up his head. Every day she called for this.

"Is Mass on time or isn't it? Usual time, or have you changed it? *Maria in Sabbato,* or some obscure hermit? White, isn't it? Well, isn't it?"

"Yes, white, Miss Hone, white."

"Who's saying the Mass? Not one of those new ones, not one of those *experimenters?*"

"Abbot Wilfrid today. But you know *that,* Miss Hone."

"Just checking. Look for Anne and Filchy and me. The hymns?"

"I don't know *that,* Miss Hone. You know I don't know that. Ask the organist that."

"Don't want *not* to know," she said. The remote and old Georgia voice trickled past. She wheezed a little and he could hear the squawk in her overtuned hearing aid setting off her dog, Filch.

She was Boldface Abbey's oldest parishioner, came to daily noon Mass wearing the proper liturgical color, brought the dog. She distrusted ornaments and especially candles. At eighty-six, she was Giles's last hope for getting the kind of

9

money he needed to do something about the decaying buildings of his monastery. He courted her this way, but he knew that she didn't think much of him. He had secured her promise of "someday," and listening to her on the phone, he imagined her as she would be shortly. There in the chapel's only cushioned pew, up front, with Filch at her feet, his chain clanking against the pine floors. She blotted out the flowers on the altar and the candles by looking at Mass through a pinhole in an index card. She had been through all of Giles's predecessors, including Abbot Hegel, who had had a celebrated fondness for the Hone family and had educated the two Hone girls and their only brother. Elizabeth, the sister, was dead, a blind poet who, in the secretarial job Abbot Hegel had got her, was paid in stocks by the infant insurance company's founder. She had later become a millionaire and left the money, when she died, to Adelaide. The two women, after their brother died, had always lived together. The rest was mystery, but the money they had was what Giles waited for.

He had the plans already drawn up for a new monastery, in fact. It was at times such as these that he took them out and studied them. Neither the absences at Office nor Father Brendan or any of it bothered him when he did this. It had something to do with God's favor at last: Giles was elected to it, it was his duty, not his burden. Brendan almost amused him; they were all amusing for the moment. He also looked at Vinnie Dano's note, which helped.

"Yes, yes, Miss Hone; yes, yes, yes, yes."

He didn't really dislike her, either, though she was like clockwork in these morning calls. She was always up and lively and she wasn't merely eccentric. Somehow at the worst

10

times he thought Miss Hone lived on the same fringes of reality that haunted him. Most of the other monks of Boldface Abbey resented her because of the way he deferred to her. But no matter. Giles thought her pleasant since the mystery in her dislike remained and he didn't know that much about her. She never really talked to him except in her present manner. She had her house on the perimeter of the property, had lived there all these years with her niece, Anne Hone, who more or less cared for her. Giles did like Anne very much and this thought prompted further deference.

He told her to take it easy. "Don't strain yourself, Miss Addie, and pray for me," he said.

She said good-by as if she had thought him condescending.

And then he was back to the study, calling down to the sacristy where Father Affirmo Biggsbee answered. Giles said, "See to Miss Hone, will you," and Affirmo, preparing for his role as master of ceremonies for noon daily Mass, replied caustically that the two of them deserved each other.

"She's deaf, and you're dumb!"

How Giles steeled himself then! He consoled himself in the presumption that this was more of the isolation one got with the purple. He wanted to be cared for, and he sighed and thought how well they had cared for him when he was outspoken enough to depose Abbot Wilfrid. Then they had cared for the forthrightness of it. Even Affirmo then said, "I see the historical spark in you." But how quickly this praise changed when he hadn't appointed Affirmo to an office in the hierarchy. Here was Affirmo, another of the brilliant persons in his charge. He had, all his life, burned the candle at both

11

ends and was always bitter about it. He was a Ph.D. at twenty-six and he had once been a good teacher in the Institute, but dry rot set in when he was forty. Giles privately believed that it was thwarted ambition. Affirmo had wanted to be an abbot, but that was another matter.

So Giles dismissed this too; he refused to consider talking to Affirmo as he had tried to talk to Father Brendan. He reread Vinnie Dano's note. He reviewed the monastery plans.

Vinnie would be there shortly, and Giles would talk about things. He smoothed down the folds in his scapular, thinking of Vinnie and what he owed him. To this point, it had always been what Vinnie owed.

It was a friendship of dependency, Giles acknowledged, smiling over the note. It was something that started when Vinnie was Giles's student at Boldface Institute at least ten years ago. Those were days when Giles had given his best to educating bright young men like Vinnie, though Vinnie brooded more than any of them and was always around to get advice. The nature of his brooding, Giles remembered with a little displeasure, was over the too ordinary matters of study and love and pleasure itself. But that had changed as much as the dependency itself, and now Giles was no longer the one who advised. Vinnie was a puzzle to him still — his finishing his time at Boldface, becoming a medical student, finally a physician. Giles remembered being completely surprised to find that he chose to settle as close by as Atlanta. He even talked of his debt to Giles, though now it had all begun to center on the oldness of things. It certainly must concern Giles's growing remoteness, and his new-found hostilities toward his work.

At any rate, Giles was thinking how well Vinnie would

12

console him. Shortly Giles would tell him once again how much he wanted to have the affection of his monks. Vinnie would be kind about it, too, though Giles knew that he was getting tired of the complaining. Vinnie never had had any use for religion, and he didn't really understand Giles's position. Last time, he had told him flatly that he could see something wrong that he wouldn't get involved in. But he also remembered the time Giles had taken with him years ago. He always told the abbot this, and he lately had said that at least he understood Giles's loneliness. He would have let his dark, subtle smile curl up like a wire, warmly suggesting that the world wasn't worth saving. And then: "Ha, ha, but you're the one, Abbot, who mustn't believe that!"

This might have been typical, and it would have been just as quickly as the two of them, at Vinnie's arrival, could get up to the abbot's room and pour themselves a drink. Here was the consolation Giles expected, and he reminded himself of it.

He went back to the desk and stuffed away the OPERATING SUGGESTIONS. He took out the journal he had kept since his ordination and, getting frightened, he wrote:

Lord, today I have already started by finding fault; what is it in me and where does the feeling come from? Will I die of it?

He chose not to be so neat as he usually was; but he had written slowly. And glancing at the pages which preceded this entry, the abbot could count the many times he had written the same words.

There *was* a faraway light. It was something which he couldn't bear to have come any closer, though it seemed sustained by his senses and to confine him strangely.

Thinking of Vinnie, he rested his arms comfortably on

13

his stomach and moved his hands up to catch them in the chain of his pectoral cross. Vinnie was talking to him and the abbot was feeling old and wise. He didn't worry about being disliked in doing God's work, neither by Affirmo nor Brendan, certainly not by Miss Hone.

TWO   FATHER OWEN CLINE, on the other hand, cared to
be liked. Being one of the few monks Miss Adelaide Hone
cared for, he was the one who usually heard her confession at
her arrival two hours before daily noon Mass, too.

She had the abbot in mind each time she spoke of "that
man" in her confession, and today it was, "I dislike that man
immeasurably, and God forgive me." She said it only half in
the confessional, curtain open. She said it loudly enough to
be heard by her niece, Anne Hone, who also was in the back
pew examining her own conscience. She would have followed her aunt there, as always.

Miss Hone then gently picked at Father Owen to see
whether she had convinced him of anything. He understood
that she thought this funny, but he felt, as well, her uncertain
hostility. He didn't talk about it because he didn't care to
have her get into one of her diatribes.

"Aren't you going to say *something?* I've done a sin, a
deep sin; I've disliked, don't you see?"

"Count on God's mercy, and . . ."

15

She was a level-headed woman in any other circumstances. She had managed her money and her time well. She was Owen's friend, and they would sit on the front porch of her bungalow on the east end of the Boldface Abbey perimeter, of an afternoon, sniffing up the tea she would have invited him to have with her. She didn't breathe well, and she wanted, of course, to be frail. She kept in her house a tank of oxygen with a long hose that ran the length of the house and then some. She wore the hose at such times, on the porch and elsewhere. The porch was round, shaped like a nipple. Detracting monks called it the "tit," her the "titmouse." She knew it and strained the folly there as if she and Owen and Anne wanted the scene to wash into oblivion. She wanted all these scenes to do so.

It was superficial for Father Owen to have pretended that he didn't know who was on the other side of the screen, too. He didn't actually listen to her, thinking instead that Anne Hone was up next. It was hot in the box, and every little thing seemed to explode in his ear.

Miss Adelaide suspected his mind was elsewhere.

"I'm sorry for my sins," she said.

He said, "I'll pray for you."

Forgetting the absolution, Owen thanked her. She patted the screen as if it were *her* absolution. That, in itself, branded the cynic on the other side of the screen. Owen knew she didn't mean what she said about the abbot. She did mean it when she invited him, finally, to tea.

He was then waiting for Miss Hone's niece.

He was a small man, now thirty, four years ordained, his head feeling buried still in what was otherwise the standard confessional. When he was here he felt as though he had always been a priest. He leaned forward with the unsuitable face of a boy, however. In that position, he might have seemed cherubic to anyone but himself and Miss Hone. Other women who delivered flowers for Saturday or Sunday Mass said his face was prophetical; since the time he had been an acolyte at ten these women told him that. "You will be a priest most certainly." And he was.

Thank God for Miss Adelaide. In the early stages of their friendship he said he disliked this image of his being a priest. She assured him that she had always, herself, deplored the formulas of those who believed in a priestly class. He then admitted that he had come to the priesthood in just this order of things. On the titmouse's front porch he had admitted, "I was impulsive; the priesthood seemed scarcely attainable." There was the silence of seminary years, he told her, Anne Hone present, looking downward, her pale skin like batiste beside Miss Adelaide's dotted Swiss.

There was the torture of coming to know that counseling and consoling and pitying were oftener self-destructive than altruistic. He disliked himself for the immediate answers that were always at his fingertips; and besides that, here there was the prevailing solitude of monastic life — not mere solitude alone, but a kind of unnamable detachment which was not the result so much of training as it was of boredom. He had pursued the priesthood breathlessly. He didn't stop to look at the prize well. This was his specter for the present: the priesthood had been too enormous a prize.

"They're all eccentrics, too. In the seminary there was Father Buzhardt who called us his little chickabiddies. What about Father Solace, another who led a national movement against purgatives?"

17

With Miss Hone's encouragement in conversations like that, and against the background of her favorite word, "vulnerable," Owen only recently admitted that he had deceived himself.

Listening now to Anne Hone's arrival, he also felt the accompanying rush of the impulse which made that deception all the more painful.

Like the rest of the monks of Boldface Abbey, Owen was puzzled by the obsessions of Abbot Giles Logan, but neither the abbot's behavior nor his supposed manias yet had for him the doom-ridden prospects about them that they had for everybody else. The disillusionment with monastic life which they found fashionable was what he wanted to avoid. He didn't blame this for his feeling. At least he thought he didn't, and that was enough to give him a little security. This part coming up he had never even told Miss Hone. The part about his real feelings.

The confessional surrounded him in left-over bulletins. Father Olaf Dotis, the novice master, would come and burn them in order to keep the infirmarian from using them to pad the urine-soaked beds of the infirm monks. That would happen eventually, but Owen's picture now was of ancient Father Joe asquat a *Sunday Messenger* photo of Jesus, the Lord's head right at Father Joe's fanny.

The confessional had a broken fan for summer, a space heater for winter. The stoles were thumbtacked to the screen frame like plundered flags.

And Anne Hone was in, breathing as if she wanted to dramatize the painlessness of her movement. She always wore that kind of perfume on Saturdays. She wore her Italian sun hat, the wide brim coming down just to darken the top of her

18

breast in shadows. She customarily averted her eyes. He imagined that her eyes were closed, and tried to see her.

"A week since my last confession. Here are my sins . . ."

Of course he didn't listen to her, either, dreading the frankness which astounded him. From the beginning she had talked like a theologian, somehow coldly numbering types and consequences as though she had already looked them up. The sins must have been few, but she commanded a sort of authenticity that complicated everything he tried to think about her. On Miss Hone's porch, at their teas, Anne seemed out of place, though she was kind to the old woman and to him. It wasn't that they weren't free to discuss whatever might have come up. Miss Hone herself loved talk about the devil; they talked about sin, too, and Miss Adelaide could go into all her details of having never, as she put it, "had a man," but she said, "and I'm not half a woman for it." This would be the time when Owen looked most awkwardly at Anne. She laughed, in control, unembarrassed. She said, "Such a shame, Aunt Addie, when you've been so long surrounded by so many men, when you've been so ready."

She winked at Owen incautiously.

He didn't understand Anne's loyalty, first of all. Understanding Miss Hone's attractiveness, he only presumed it was loyalty though. Miss Hone had educated her, but Anne had her own money. She had her striking clothes as well; her thin smooth face growing, like a Van Gogh light, out of whatever she had on. And this impelled from something underneath that was mostly smell. Her master's degree in languages she held up as if it represented cosmic detachment.

He had never been alone with her except in the confessional. This was like all of his other duties. It made him feel childish.

Though Anne herself whispered to him with a caution she supposed was only right. For the moment it was important to her that she had gone to Europe when she was nineteen. There it was a matter of dealing with her own provinciality, being a Georgian, a small-town American going away to get all the experience that her two aunts had convinced her father was necessary for sophistication. She understood that she learned what she was supposed to and had studied the languages she knew with the spirit that made each part of her knowledge exciting and simple. Now, there weren't any problems she thought about. She had done her traveling with great intensity, noting everything. She thought that she had acquired a disposition that needed nothing but the challenge of classifying what she knew. It hadn't always been that way, of course. But what she knew, she supposed, was this: a subtle contentment. For in France she had enjoyed the old and the new. In Spain the superior old, where both her ideas and her faith had been crystallized by the church's insistence that specious philosophies most often hide in expectation. This was, in a way, her sustenance, though it had come strangely through a growing attachment to her senses.

Anne simply enjoyed being a part of things, then, being aware of all the movements which she was capable of. She attached this happiness to God's benevolence.

How it happened exactly puzzled her; it wasn't important. She had got tired of it, and what she learned from her aunt was that she could grow old holding on to the things she had learned. It pleased her to make distinctions. Miss Hone helped this along and Anne told herself that it was right. She also persisted in putting aside other things which, meantime, weren't important either.

Certainly she only suspected that Owen Cline was feeling what he always felt. He had come to like being near her this way, and while she was confessing to him, he was reliving moments in his novitiate class when he and the other four novices of that year listened to the novice master, Father Olaf Dotis, himself, making the proper admonition:

"My dear young men, we are first going to spend a long time on the Holy Rule of our dear founder. There is the matter, first, of the vows, which are poverty, obedience . . . and the other one."

"Chastity, Father?"

"Yes, the other one."

Clammering through an entire year of lectures and conferences, the old monk couldn't bring himself to say the word.

"Furthermore, you young men must learn the folly of looking upon the face of a . . . uh . . . woman."

Owen was trying to see more of Anne's face. He knelt softly nearer the voice. He straddled the metal prongs of the front of the broken electric fan. He felt the hardness of its knobs and the single smooth spot at its old-fashioned middle: GE. He was moving against the surface there.

Father Owen was feeling especially close to her. An unnamed god was politely holding up the world for a change. There were specters of sound, rushing sound, and the heart of a better reality approaching him. He moved delicately as he always had, as in the seminary where there would always have been someone to hear in the next bed over.

Then he said, "Oh God." He sat up quickly, worrying that Anne had heard.

"Father," she asked, "are you still there? Father, is something the matter?"

He wildly imagined answering her truthfully. But wildly said the words of absolution. He heard her go away. He sat with his head reeling far ahead of his body, and attaching significance only to the haste with which he had done it this time. The irresponsibility there.

He pulled at his underwear, drawing his hands underneath the cassock through his pockets. He was feeling the heat, all the explosions. He imagined the displeasure of Father Olaf Dotis, of voices calling through him, falling at last on a deadened spirit.

But then he didn't care, tasting in his own saliva the adolescence which he saw in himself and which remained as if there would never be anything new in his life.

And so he left the confessional, avoiding seeing her, rushing toward his room where he would customarily change his clothes. He took all the quietest routes, not wanting to be seen, but he heard Father Affirmo Biggsbee calling from the back porch. He rocked there stolidly and said, "Did the titmouse tell you anything new today, ha, ha?"

"She raped two truck drivers, what else!"

It wasn't funny to Affirmo and he puffed his cigarette, and posed like a draftsman's pencil. This man's body was a construction of right angles, and whatever he did, it was never elastic. For the time being, the arms were supporting the great weight of a cigarette at ninety degrees. He was an extension of the chair.

The porch was a long one which ran the full back of the monastery. It cut off at one point like a bridge that was out. There, the lay of the porch was wider and chairs had been set. Of a summer, it was the most comfortable part of the monastery complex, having the breeze from the north and the heavy lurching branches of five nearby oaks for shade. For most, it was also a hallowed place since it had been the location where hundreds of now-dead monks usually congregated after supper when the regimen was stricter. Oftener they had used it for chapter meetings, also, and May Devotions. There, under the mimosa, and decaying and full of stout weeds, was the place where Father Cyril Drewe, old as God, daily emptied his slop jar.

Owen sidled near Affirmo, just for conversation, just for cover, and sat on the rim of another rocker, a darker shade of green. He edged the trunk of his body off.

Affirmo looked at him quizzically. He had a way with this sort of thing, mostly stirring conversation with it, appearing omniscient. Besides being Abbot Giles's loudest critic, he was also a jealous man. And tradition was that this alienated him from most of the monks except those few who didn't mind giving him the illusion that he possessed them; or those, like Father Owen Cline, who managed to remain detached from him and thus keep him intrigued. Affirmo was interested in Owen's dealings with Adelaide Hone.

And for now he smiled weakly. It was also tradition that he never picked at his confreres without ulterior motives. As he was growing old, as well, he had developed the normal preoccupation with trivia that got to monks who no longer had much to do. For this he was bitter, recognizing it.

He disliked Adelaide Hone as much as any of them,

23

though his latest fixation remained with Abbot Giles. Being a historian of the Renaissance particularly, he proposed to see a distinct resemblance between Abbot Giles and Machiavelli's Prince. He researched it; confronting the abbot with it, he said, "How many aliens are you going to import this week, and how many of your enemies are you going to put in high places after that?"

"I have three categories," Affirmo told Owen. His cameo face sparkled. When he moved his hands forward they emerged out of spotless French cuffs from underneath his cassock sleeves, like a magician's.

"The first category has to do with taking your enemies and putting them in high places, as you know — you know this of course — that he once despised foolish Father Dorian. Remember? Now Father Dorian is the sub-prior. You see, don't you, what I mean? Of course you see . . ."

He went on, leaning forward, "But take me, for example. Don't you also remember how I assisted him in getting elected? I was the one who said there is something historical about him. Remember that? You don't see *me* in any high places."

The cigarette flashed almost fast enough to have hidden Father Affirmo's face in its movement.

"I could at least have been made sub-prior."

"Whatever you say, Father." Owen swished the bottom of his cassock and looked away. He went back to the earlier thoughts. The dark came and went again. It was carried now in the tightness of his nerves. Last, it was also carried in the senility of Affirmo's remarks, and Owen was getting angry. The archivist was going on about Miss Hone's deal-

24

ings with the abbot, and that she was better off dead than that. Owen stared at him ungraciously until he had stopped. And then Owen retraced his steps. He stood and said goodby and left the priest. He wandered limply along the ramp of the back porch and finally to his cell on the fourth floor of the west wing. There, led by the darkness he preferred, he thought of Anne Hone further.

From the first time he met her (and that must have been one of his earliest days in the priesthood) he had dealt with her this way. But not that merely. Now Owen had begun to fear what he couldn't explain about it, though urges which he didn't want to control had already taken over as usual.

He sat on the floor against the wall in the dark, pulled off his underwear. He disrobed the rest of the way, listening to his heartbeat which thumped frantically against the excitement. The edge of what he felt also gave him an impulse to think of himself being, someday, like Father Affirmo. But, worse, of staying the way he was now.

THREE   OUTSIDE IN THE GARDEN, the voices of monks waiting for daily noon Mass and taking advantage of the summertime which freed them from teaching, went up in a game of Jarts. Both the hour and its almost natural laziness perplexed them. The older ones, guilty not to be busy at something, mowed the lawn. Father Olaf Dotis, the novice master, burned debris from under the crawling wisteria bushes, in and out from behind them, against the pitches of some of the Jarts players who had no aim. In his worn sweater and baseball cap, he was poor and industrious beside his confreres, who tied the fronts of their scapulars behind them with the backs of their scapulars and looked like nineteenth-century women playing tennis.

All the action beyond was dominated by the deep-voiced and booming former abbot, Wilfrid Coogan, who curled up his arms, enjoying the morning. He flung the weighted arrow the whole twenty feet that it took to put it in Father Olaf's debris.

The two men confronted each other with an allowance

which meant that neither was angry, but that each felt the other had something better to do.

Summers were always like this. There was a tiredness reflecting itself in the difficult ease with which the monks relaxed. The year had been treacherous, not merely because they had been forced to deal with Giles Logan's second year as abbot, but because, as well, they couldn't handle the new breed of student at Boldface Institute. Though there were few good students, it was almost as if the monks preferred stupid ones because it made fewer worries (Father Affirmo, for example, hadn't changed the content of his classes in thirty years). But with the stupidity of the students there was a nonchalance which also challenged old prescriptions and dress codes and religious duties. People like Father Olaf, who for forty years had taught Latin and algebra and maintained that the first duty of a teacher was "to be there," had dropped out altogether.

Each was aware of the other's adjustment to this sort of thing, and they laughed about it.

They laughed at Abbot Wilfrid's shots. He, these days, spent almost all his time in the basement where he worked exclusively with his movie equipment.

The young monks who were opponents to Father Philip, Wilfrid's teammate, and himself, laughed especially according to allegiances. It was a race of age against youth, but no one said it. And instead, the younger men in the game pretended to be sympathetic. They really didn't know how to treat a deposed abbot.

It was one of the younger monks who raised his arms like a projectionist and asked the abbot what sort of film he was making these days.

27

Wilfrid supposed the condescension there. He lifted up his own arm and neighed a little. He had a habit of laughing only with the highest part of his voice, and anybody who didn't know him would never have been able to match his laugh with his speaking voice. This was a joke.

The deposed abbot slapped his overweight belly.

"I thought I would make a promotion movie, a vocation movie," he said. "We could, for instance, get the monks out in their habits pitching hay in the field. Beautiful picture of monastic life! It would attract new monks."

The younger priests laughed. They all laughed, all those standing around now. They laughed as the old abbot wound his fingers in a curl and returned their laughs with his own smile.

"Monks don't pitch hay anymore, Abbot. They pitched hay in the fourteenth century."

"Then we ought to restore the fourteenth century."

The gentle old man crossed himself. He looked upward. His face was lively and annoyed. He said nothing more. He kept standing there until someone said, "Is this game going to get off the ground or not?"

They continued.

Father Brendan Price then came with Myrtis Crawford from around the side of the church and stood with her near the edge of the garden. He did this every day and they knew he was there. As they remained ambivalent about him and Myrtis, they were also unconvinced that Brendan was afflicted worse than she was. For him it was almost a private triumph. He was saying good-by to her in the usual manner.

And Myrtis had on a dress she had had for years. She always wore this dress on Saturdays, a floral print of begonias that still had its summery look and its shoulder pads from the 40s. She had black hair, which she bobbed, too, though she had never dyed it and gray was showing. Myrtis had her cigarettes, and so her attractive straight teeth were yellowing with the stains.

Yes, there she was for all the world to see. At the proper distance they might all have admitted that she was as elegant as she had always been, the lankness carried like a duty, and then especially engaged in contrast to crazy old Brendan with his fat body, his bald head. He was standing there grinning, with his hands in front of him.

The truth was that, after that business with Abbot Giles in the morning, he rallied quickly. He didn't just then continue what he always did as soon as he woke up in the morning. And so the monks who played Jarts didn't know that Brendan was sober. They knew he drank to keep the demons away.

But now he felt, with the abbot, the constraints of a new honesty. He believed in demons who hide their effects in weakness. He felt sure it was the reason that Myrtis was able to deal with him and the abbot wasn't. Her simplicity astounded him, believing in demons. No monk tolerated this in him, or the truth, or any of the follies in his present fear of getting old. That was it: he wanted to be thirty again. But Myrtis didn't care about that. He was comfortable having her know, remembering that even the first time they had gone to bed together he had seen the meaninglessness of his own intelligence beside her sentimentality. She talked to him in well-known baby talk.

In the distance, Father Affirmo Biggsbee kept rocking on the porch where Owen Cline had left him. He kept motioning for Brendan now, rocking sensitively, enjoying the motion, and finally the company, of his closest associate. He smirked in mediating eye contact with Father Phineas Rapp who had joined him on the porch.

He said, "Damn Myrtis Crawford. Again."

In all the years they had been together Brendan and Affirmo never talked about Myrtis. It was unspeakable to Affirmo, but he liked Brendan. And when this priest joined them on the porch Affirmo easily permitted his friend's darker composure to dominate. They were all uninterested in Jarts.

They said nothing until Myrtis had gone off like some aging queen in a boat. Brendan, towering and young and old at the same time, stared after her; then finally at Phineas, the community organist and musician, who was chewing a toothpick. He had a habit, as well, of taking little wisps of hair and pulling them into a cushion at the ends of his fingers. He rubbed the hair as if it were a button.

When he was younger Phineas had been a fair musician and they had sent him off for serious piano study, but since Boldface Abbey had no music department, he had spent the last twenty years giving private lessons to children and to a few Institute students who were always beginners. He had never had a respectable student.

At any rate, he and Affirmo both despised Abbot Giles.

"Silly nonsense," Phineas said, referring to the Jarts game. "Haven't they got anything better to do?" He sucked on the toothpick, leaning forward, stretching his shoulders out on his arms; a wrestler, looking quickly for space.

Since the comment was characteristic, the other two ignored him. Father Brendan at last took out his flask to this.

30

"Cheers."

Affirmo averted his eyes. Phineas, horrified, told him that he was killing himself.

Brendan, of course, drank to these words: "There is a God, you know."

And so the morning was going in all but the token abridgments of its importance. These monks sat on and said little more.

Until Father Brendan first saw the sullenness which overtook his dear friends. They all liked this point in the day.

They watched the Jarts game end. They heard the bell ring for daily noon Mass, and these monks, and the others, filed in with degrees of interest to what was the only part of the monastic observance they still took seriously. And yet with its delights and its invariables they held it in contempt. Each had auxiliary enterprises, to be sure, not the least of which was their amusement with Adelaide Hone and her index cards. All waited for those days when it would be Father Brendan's turn to be principal celebrant; he subtly blessed her with the third finger of his right hand up.

Abbot Giles arrived, vested. No one paid him any attention. He smiled while the last of the sweaty Jarts players hurried past. Giles hadn't lost his earlier disposition yet. He wasn't trying to explain a more complete awareness of his touch either. He fingered the amice strings, and his stare remained as he nodded to Father Owen Cline, arriving, and to Father Affirmo, master of ceremonies, who said, "For Godssakes don't mutter today. Enunciate like a prelate."

The Mass was concelebrated; those who participated did it together and they gathered at the entrance of the sanctuary

31

where the candles had softly penetrated both the darkness of the old chapel and the musty smell of its frescoed walls. The organ blower whirred behind the storage door where it was located. The door opened and closed with air leakage, and Father Phineas, at the organ, mumbled at the imagined detractor who must have taken the nail out of the door. He didn't fix the door; he didn't go up there, and instead sat quietly with his copy of *The Prayers of Kierkegaard*.

Miss Hone had arranged herself comfortably, and she knelt with her ready index card. Filch slept at her feet, and Anne Hone, with attention, assisted the old lady in tuning her hearing aid. Anne laughed sweetly to have set the dog off, and drew Father Owen's attention. The rest looked, though in the humor of the event she had reserved eye contact for him. Her thin face flushed as she shrugged.

Miss Hone's white dress matched the antependium on the altar.

The entrance. Hymn 362.

Father Phineas set it romantically and offered an obbligato. They sang, "In Christ there is no east nor west."

He had a faint smile and set up the *positif* with special cadences of "Dixie." They heard it at the ends of the cadences, but this didn't matter, and when they didn't keep up the tempo, he left them behind.

For the incensation he would play "Smoke Gets in Your Eyes."

The mass was a conglomerate of adjustments that the community had made to the Second Vatican Council liturgy and rubrics. Particularly difficult for Abbot Wilfrid. It took extra time because the former abbot was of the old school, though it was a pleasure for the small congregation who remembered him favorably and came to Mass especially when

32

he was main celebrant. In a way, he represented their grievances in his avoidance of new things.

Miss Hone and Anne were pleased to have his sure hand lifting the host.

In fact, Miss Adelaide and Anne, in contrast to the monks, were distant, and at least Father Owen Cline watched their reverence. The old woman's palsied hands were rough, the veins popping out like telephone cords hidden along a chair rail. Her hands were visibly strong at this distance. She stroked the dog as though it were not merely a pet.

A dog in church, to Owen's suddenly cynical eye, was perfect. Miss Hone was also perfect, and what he imagined about Anne Hone drew him away. He could see only her lips under the Italian sun hat, except at moments when she looked forward pensively, resting her chin in a handkerchiefed hand. She touched the handkerchief, like smelling salts, to her nose.

She did pray. Her mind was on the ceremony and on the dust motes which the open back door let in like flies. But with the further lure of their balance they held her imagination as if to become spirals, brush strokes, thin wires, the forms of creatures with uncertain bodies. She was looking at Father Owen trustfully at last, but thinking him silly.

When noon daily Mass was over, Owen went to the vestibule where he customarily said good-by to them. Others did as well, and Miss Hone, still gathering her paraphernalia and edging Filch out of his sleep, ritually flashed her hand all around Owen's shoulders and embraced him. For the first time, he thought himself transposing that gesture to Anne Hone, though only swiftly aware of the older woman's frailty.

"And don't forget afternoon tea," Miss Hone said.

FOUR   ABBOT GILES was in the vestibule, too, and grop-
ing to do whatever would have been Miss Hone's pleasure
this time. The awkwardness of playing her game left him
sweating even though it was also routine here.

His monks avoided him. She grunted at him.

"You."

Then it was a matter of his getting back to his room
where what he earlier felt was revitalized. He hadn't ignored
the coldness of their treatment of the Mass. Phineas's music
never escaped him. Nor Father Affirmo's brutal movements
with the ceremony. But Giles knew that his own frame of
mind had dwindled too. How could he feel responsible?

Actually he would laugh at Phineas.

He could laugh at all of them.

He especially had Father Brendan Price in mind then —
Brendan, who more than anybody used to be able to convince him that what he most needed in life was a sense of
humor. In those days Brendan was a happy man and his
adjustments were private. Brendan always laughed, his bald

head the symbol of an almost sacred will to be amused. Giles laughed at him at his most drunken, for example, when he would come in late at night, having been out with Myrtis undoubtedly, march to the infirmary toilet on the first floor, and wake the crankiest of the infirm monks, Justin Loem, who raved and swore that somebody was banging the toilet seat only to torment him. And Brendan was.

Justin lay awake waiting to be aroused and Giles couldn't resist thinking that Father Brendan was serving a special purpose in giving the old man something to complain about.

What about the complaining? It might have been a joy.

Brendan often said, "The first weakness the demons deliver us to is paranoia. What do you think monks invented prayer for?"

Giles said, "Ha, ha." And stood in front of the mirror and touched the top of his scapular, traced the lines of the red piping that ran the length of the opening there.

He arranged the cross nicely and turned sideways so that he could see the red zuchetto better. He arched his eyebrows up and opened his mouth to look at his teeth, the only part of himself that he thought attractive.

He had a fascination with brushing his teeth. It came, he imagined, from childhood when his mother had insisted that clean teeth were the only thing that a man could count on till he died. She always said that Giles was ugly, and he thought it too. As long as he squinted at the mirror, he could arrange the highlights in his appearance so that they were more agreeable. He remembered the first of his abbatial garbs and the excitement of having them arrive. At that, the community happily assisted him in arranging them. They

35

told him that he looked a prince: it was the tradition of the founding abbot. He had liked it, and the first ceremonies held him in thrall to the supposed dignity of his High Office. It was a great pleasure for him to have designed his coat of arms as well. And he recalled how thoughtfully he gathered up monastic crests and mottoes; he solicited them, in fact, from all the monks, and filed them according to the donors' preferences. The one thing he insisted on was that the coat of arms represent something from their history, and, too, that it have some mention of Vinnie Dano. He imagined Vinnie, then, to have stood in for all his former students, a representative, he said, of his close friends at Boldface Institute. He supposed they disliked that.

Vinnie was on his mind.

He didn't want to open his eyes all the way. He was feeling the silence and thinking of the particles of air which might have been delivering his thoughts. It was like his childhood when he used to say: if the tree leaf doesn't move over there three times in the next moment, you will die. He thought: so long as the light remains, I won't die.

The coat of arms represented the magnitude of his work. He wanted Vinnie Dano to know this again. That's what they would talk about first when Vinnie arrived: the two dolphins which are goodness, the turning lines below them which stand for truth. They intersect.

The abbot's dark hair, in the silence, and in the partial darkness, wasn't commonplace by the distance that now he assumed, or by the absence of a clear face which his squinting allowed. He didn't mind this part; the isolated hairline was even splendid.

Here was his game, putting his face slowly to the point

36

at which he began to see his eyes in the mirror. Then his nose. Finally he could look at himself full-length, and the game ended.

Giles wrote in his journal:

Do I, therefore, believe?

There were shadows up from outside objects moving past the window. These were images of birds, or reflections from automobile windshields. The light was reflecting them.

He was thinking of his duties and of his formulas for his duties; of his duties' duties, of having brought on his duties, and then of having failed at them. Abbot Wilfrid Coogan haunted him as the tradition of former abbots haunted him.

The church itself haunted him.

Boldface Abbey *was* falling apart. This had its roots, of course, in Giles's uncertainty of what monasticism ought really to be. How was he, as an abbot, to guide his monastery? An old question, and one which he was certain had worried the founders and administrators of religious institutes since antiquity. But now it was his question.

He wanted to examine himself against people like Father Brendan who also said that their lives made them protectors of unseen dignities which discipline guaranteed.

The goal was, in any case, peace. There wasn't any for Giles. There was peace for Brendan.

Giles thought about the founder, Alcuin Hegel, doing what the book of customs celebrated most of all: answering the front door in his overalls. This was his kind of charisma, generating, first, the love of his monks.

There was the other legend of his having lost his abbatial ring gathering eggs for his monks in the hen house.

Abbot Hegel once prevented a fire with the sweep of his hand. He had planted trees, built duck ponds; the missals were his, the flowers, the vestments, the designs of all the property.

The room itself carried the old man's spell. The desk was bolted to the floor in the place where Abbot Hegel had ordered it. Giles had to step across the phone lines if he was to keep the phone on his desk. And the desk was defaced with Abbot Hegel's ink stains. The ceiling paint had never been changed, nor the wall-coloring. The room had been painted in the days of calcimized paint and neither latex nor oil would cover. Small prongs of paint were always falling. Giles often woke up with them in his eyes.

But now the new monastery. He expected thinking about it to restore his confidence. Once gripped, the thought soothed him as it usually did. He fingered the plans, and he thumbed them with a fast glide that was getting electric. In the middle of this, he wished that he could dispose himself also to accept everything his senses told him. He liked the touch of blueprint paper.

He was drawing his eyes out of focus again. The shapes in front of him stretched into total forms. He didn't mind these forms. He imagined Abbot Hegel in procession, walking the promenade around the back of the church. The acolytes were bowing to him. They shoved the umbrellina above. The incense pots glided like lazy drying laundry. Abbot Hegel was carrying the monstrance, offering the blessing in his expensive brocade cope.

It was an Easter celebration, the church brilliantly lighted, candles seeming puzzle pieces, the ceremony full, chant corporate, schola trained. Positive.

38

Then Giles raised his own hand in a blessing. Thrice he blessed the mirror and himself, though he supposed that the blessing meant very little. It had been whittled away like everything else. The bare stalls of the monks which used to call forth pleas and reparation had only the hasty stolen melodies of the Anglican psalmody, and oftener Father Phineas's adaptations of popular songs. It was the same with the abbacy.

The past was better.

Giles imagined other nearly transcendent examples of this world of substance. His imagination intensified at having never really known them. Nor did he even know the founding abbot, who had died in 1930. If the truth were known, Abbot Hegel left behind the only fine things remaining at Boldface Abbey.

I am the abbot, Giles thought.

He noted quickly on the scratch pad:

the problem of complaining must be solved
and
Father Brendan's drinking and Myrtis Crawford
and Father Affirmo's tongue and Father
Phineas's music

This, also, was what the next community conference would be:

There's something wrong with us, my dear confreres. We're not happy. I don't mean that *I'm* not happy, I mean that *we're* not.

This abbot was quickly consumed with the instinct to believe that it couldn't be otherwise. He partially imagined being led to his state by God, or at least by Abbot Hegel's inspiration. It perplexed him that he too readily shifted allegiances, but that went inward, becoming an obscure but nearly predestined notion of even newer wisdom.

It wouldn't last, he thought; and where the hell was Vinnie Dano?

FIVE   SO, TWO IN THE AFTERNOON. He sat and mumbled to himself, a tired joy, perhaps, as though he were going into a classroom to teach for the first time. Giles, weeks before, had called a chapter meeting for this time. Only now the agenda could concern all the things on his note pad. He had the OPERATING SUGGESTIONS ready.

He imagined this time convincing them with an honest approach. He said that he would just talk about it, and he left his room casually. He walked the hallway quietly. This hallway the brightest place hereabouts, its twenty windows still holding the opaque glass of Abbot Hegel's time. The fissures in the glass made curious designs on the other side of the wall where the second-floor cells were.

Hello to everybody, and at the end of the hallway, Father Brendan stopped him. Brendan was more than usually pensive. His breath was acid, and Giles didn't say anything. He was calm, and Brendan said, "About this morning; look, we've got some things to settle. I talked about it to Myrtis."

Giles supposed some climax of decision had come.

"I'm sorry, Father Brendan, I just hadn't thought about it well enough."

"I can't stop with Myrtis; I wanted to tell you that." His face was absorbed in the heavy sunlight. Giles wanted to see him.

"We went about it the wrong way," Giles said. "I mean, I should simply have told you what I thought."

"You did."

"I mean I should have told you that I think it must really stop. You need to work on your observance."

Brendan said, "You try too hard, son."

His eyes through the sun were pleading. Giles trusted the light. He didn't have to avoid looking at the priest.

"Don't you see," Brendan said, "that I've been a monk too long? Remember the old things . . . just don't do me favors and feel responsible."

And somehow Giles could feel the machinery of things changing again. No one could want this, he thought; no one could operate under this restriction. Brendan was absolutely clear-headed. Giles swore that even now this priest kept the same distance that gave him his extreme dignity. When he got to the chapter room Giles had shifted his disposition another notch.

"I've called this meeting to discuss . . ."

He was holding up the OPERATING SUGGESTIONS. He did it nervously, confusing them. They laughed at first. Father Affirmo grunted and stood up. He was at the door to leave.

"One damn thing after another!"

"Affirmo, please please sit down. Father Affirmo, sit down!"

The room was cavernous and used to be a dormitory before the monks had begun sleeping in private cells. In Abbot Hegel's time, twenty-four beds had been there. These beds were mere cots with featherbed mattresses. The floors were worn with holes made by the unferruled brass bedsteads. Some of the holes were large enough to engulf a chair leg.

On one wall hung enormous portraits of all the abbots. They were done in the lifetime of the single painter of the community, an old monk who painted with the help of one of those machines that reflect on the wall. Abbot Giles's portrait, the newest, had him on the throne, mitred, with a book in his hand. His feet were on a stool. There had been no dissuading the painter, who chose the photograph, from copying the head only and filling in the rest.

The ceiling made the room seem twice its size. It was tin and filigreed. Elsewhere the paint was chipping too fast for the novices to keep the floor clear of it. The paint bits checkered the floor, and it was Father Owen Cline who sat in his place and imagined that, just around his foot, they made a mask with four ears. At the nearest juncture, dogs copulating.

The rest of the monks were gathering slowly, and the room as slowly filled with the sounds of woolen habits swishing in various stages of disrepair. Some of them had been newly laundered, and others not, like Father Leo's, filthy with food stains, shaving cream, his own saliva. Father Leo was both infirmarian and refectorian. He had two remedies for sickness: if the ailment was above the waist, an aspirin; if below, an enema.

Owen watched them carefully. He watched Father Cyril

Drewe, next, waddling in and checking to see that no one who was not a chapter member was there. He assumed that chapter meetings meant that there would be a *scrutinium* on one of the novices. His invariable question came out of the deafness and senility that had set in a quarter of a century before: How much Latin has the boy had? Pertinence meant nothing to him.

And the abbot also kept watching intently, reducing his disdain even more. Because he could think of hundreds of times when he had been angry in this way. Because on the one hand, any one of them could have objectively been tainted, and, on the other, to see them this way, all together and almost collectively a perfect picture of human nature, was enough to shame his feeling.

The younger ones, in contrast to the older men, were apt promises of a future less sordid; but they were colorless beside Cyril (now he was humming the Austrian National Anthem).

Giles thought of the preferences of the young ones too. They talked of "communication." One spoke, for example, of his own Theory of Dichotomosis which, he said, held that the "true relationship between human parties is one of adjustment to projected self."

Oh, how Giles preferred the old monks, watching their habits of expression as though they had been ground out of those fixed processes which, all in all, seemed an electric part of a better year. Some of them, like Affirmo, smoked so many cigarettes that it was impossible to imagine them without smoke in their faces. And there Father Brendan sat, the true representative of it all, not a loathsome man, not misguided, peaceful. There was no caution; he was finishing off a vulgar joke.

44

Giles touched the OPERATING SUGGESTIONS even less severely and swept them aside. He stood and called the roll. The *adsums* filled the air, which was already sour with cigarette smoke. The wind of camaraderie cut through it, smoke being merely the motto.

Giles said, then, "Forget the OPERATING SUGGESTIONS." He said, "What I really meant is that, today, we're going to discuss the plans for a new monastery . . . and why not?" He made it up. He tried to smile. It was as if he had betrayed his hand, and he felt himself slipping. Then a profound affection came on. He felt strangely lured to penitence.

"The monastery is the thing," Giles said. "New buildings are our hope in this community, a fresh look, and just imagine what it could do for us."

Affirmo said, "What is this, a travesty or something?"

Well, chapter meetings were always ludicrous anyhow. The monks deplored them more than any of the monastery routines. It took their time, though few, of a summer, had that much pressing them otherwise. It was just that, somehow, they represented an ordeal with the abbot. They called them his follies. This against the ambivalence that Affirmo was spotting exactly. Somewhere the two poles of Giles's nature kept him from settling on a middle road that would allow him to make an honest statement of his ideas. He had never done it, not since the first few weeks of his new election to the office. At these moments he felt his authority slip most, almost as if they might predictably dismiss the meeting as another folly. They did, of course, already.

The faces were bemused, if not simply distrustful. It was the kind of feeling they always had had for Abbot Wilfrid. It was what Giles himself had felt for the former abbot.

Affirmo said it best. "Silly thing, another damn meeting, this one about a nonexistent monastery. I've other things to do. And what about the money, Abbot? What about that!"

"Well, Miss Hone . . ."

They roared with laughter.

"What I want to know," said Affirmo, "is what the hell the real reason is. What's this meeting *for?*"

Affirmo liked the agitation. He led the expectant faces at last. They wouldn't be contained by indecision, and Giles understood. It made him angrier. He put his head down.

"The real truth," he said, "is that most of you are against me, and all I'm trying to do is keep the place together."

"What's *wrong* with the place?"

Affirmo was standing with one hand on his hip. The elbow was out like a triangle. He stared splendidly.

They mumbled for parallels in the book of customs. The theologians talked about the Holy Rule.

Affirmo said, "As the abbot goes, so goes the monastery!"

And Giles felt absolutely foolish. It was an incredible pettiness that they argued this way. Not just now, but for years it had been the prevailing spirit of things. Giles supposed it had something to do with their perfect security. He and Brendan had talked of its being a country club atmosphere; they were petty lords of a feudal kingdom. A thousand-acre estate on Georgia land, procured in the past by a man whose ideals and authorities belonged to the nineteenth century. They still had the traditions. A man came to the monastery, he stayed there for seven years before he was completely trusted, then he made his vows, tried through those years in a thousand small and inconsequential ways.

46

Then he was free. Boldface Abbey just hadn't kept up, or perhaps it had kept up too well. At least, in Giles's mind, it hadn't grown. And they were still comfortable in the old. Old in the formulas which specified that the true heart was somehow entitled to the leisure which came with proper loyalty. That loyalty was undefined, if not indefensible, especially when now it seemed only to have come from a deeply buried complacency. Where was their faith? He saw the contradiction in himself, too, wanting the old way with things. Here was what he couldn't find the words to say, and he himself disliked those ineffectual methods which he had adopted when he first took office. He had even abolished the rule that they must stand up when he came into a room.

"Well, however unfortunate it is, I am the abbot."

The silence was startling to everybody.

"And I'm going to tell you what's wrong. Here's what's wrong."

He scattered the poor beleaguered OPERATING SUGGESTIONS on the table soberly.

"It's not God, not Boldface Institute, not prayer. It's shaving cream . . . and underwear."

"Shaving cream and underwear, ha, ha, ha, ha!"

"Abbot, that's unfair."

The silence became collective breathing.

Father Affirmo said he had in mind the Inquisition.

As for the other monks, it was a matter of superbly suppressed astonishment.

Until Father Brendan Price, in the far corner, listening carefully, his face sorrowful all along, spoke from his chair, "This is pettiness," he said. "This is like hearing nuns' confessions, like being stoned with popcorn." He wasn't sure

47

himself whether he meant that to be funny. He looked at Giles, though, who was showing his pleading eyes, and eyes shot from enduring his notion of the hostility which was there and not there at the same time. Brendan looked at him deeply and for a long time.

The monks waited.

They weren't accustomed to having Brendan approach the spiritual issues; they assumed he had condemned himself long ago. He hadn't talked in chapter for ten years at least.

He said, "Well, I assume that you all know my sins."

He thought loftily, no sudden desire to have escaped a duty he almost felt compelled to assume for his own protection. Giles's eyes followed him, Brendan saw. He remembered a young man who once came to him in the middle of the night frightened of the terrible silence in the monastery. Giles Logan, a month and a half after his arrival, had wanted to quit because he couldn't stand the quietness. Giles wept that his own helpless desire to be alone couldn't possibly be contained this way. Brendan told him to take a cold shower. He got Giles hot milk from the infirmary and told him jokes. The catlike face had seemed then to turn with a certain decision, and from then on Giles always looked his best when his conviction showed.

Here the abbot's face had regained an old truth, it seemed. He might not even have been ugly but for the foment in his voice.

"The abbot is right, you know."

Brendan stood. He twisted a pipe cleaner nervously under his fingernails as if cleaning them. The nervous habit secured his shaking hands. He told them that he knew what they thought of *him*. He had to bring Myrtis up.

48

"But there's something between Myrtis and me that I can't explain and won't give up. I'd die first. And, you know, its absence is what's making this place dismal. I'm not talking about love."

He looked at Giles especially, noted the nearly contemptuous expressions of the young monks, Affirmo's shock, Father Olaf Dotis's evading face.

"No, there's the fundamental issue of loneliness. We're crying out when we aren't happy. That isn't pagan. We attack each other to live with ourselves."

This had been in there a long time. He was going now.

"We do laugh, but we don't know why we have a right to laugh. Why we should, in fact. This laughter is false."

It was time to tell them how Myrtis and he had discovered their contentment.

He wanted to say no, no it wasn't the way anymore than love was the way.

"We can't even admit that we're men!"

He demanded attention now.

"Myrtis is beautiful. She's there and touches me, you see. But what we do isn't the horror that you imagine. It hasn't broken any rule because it's freed me. What we do tells me that I'm here, for Godssakes. I so love God for it."

He was almost crying and saying that he wasn't sure of the pertinence but that he had to say it and that it hadn't produced what he wanted. Myrtis was the dearest thing, but he had held all those jobs in the past, said all the prayers, fallen little by little into that proper security.

"But finally there was nothing. Do you think I can really stand myself? My sins are left. The problem, if you want to know, is the long-ignored futility."

49

He faltered, watching the abbot himself become ill at ease; they stared at him like losers at a bingo party. They pitied him superbly.

Father Affirmo said, "I don't believe in sensitivity sessions."

Father Phineas said, "Yes, Father Brendan, your dirty laundry belongs in the confessional."

But Brendan was saying, "Maybe worse, it's your stone-cold consciences."

They quailed at this insult with continued disbelief. They sat while Brendan fled the room and, when he was gone, it was Father Affirmo who reluctantly suggested that they must somehow get help for him.

They didn't talk about this. They left this to the abbot, they said, and Abbot Giles, somehow too embarrassed to continue, but too moved to lose the moment from his own thoughts, had let it go by.

He did know that he felt clumsy in the final prayer. He fidgeted with the OPERATING SUGGESTIONS, while those who were deaf and those who were blind and lame poked at nearby confreres for a translation of events.

This gathering dispersed in further silence. Some of them smiled and nudged each other alongside the youngest monk of all who was giggling. The rest of the observance, like spiriting raw electricity, plummeted through the air and went away.

SIX   THAT LEFT OWEN CLINE there alone. He watched
them leave, even catching the abbot's eye as if to compliment
him. For the moment, he couldn't dislike Giles.

He remembered the abbot from other days, a young and
vibrant man. Maybe a little simple-minded. Only that,
because he had had visions, they all said, and he even appeared guileless as those times when, in dealing with former
abbot, Wilfrid, he bluntly and dutifully spoke of things as
they were.

Owen remembered talking to Giles. Before he was ordained, this priest could seek out his future abbot and they
would have moments of candor. The abbot would, for example, have something to say about Abbot Wilfrid: "He stays
down there in the basement, goddamn it, and there's not
even anybody appointed to sell cemetery plots. There are
bodies on top of bodies out there."

Or else this one, the commonest complaint: "That mis-
erable old man has spent two hundred dollars on a pro-
jector."

Owen might then have cheered Giles's forthrightness after all.

The total silence was for that moment frightening. Owen's hearing resumed its former explosions. His body was lank and he felt an added staleness. Even here, his body dominated him and he leaned back on the chair.

The chapter meeting lingered. He thought of Father Affirmo and the hatred this priest couldn't spare. He saw Brendan in a special light and thought the doubt he spoke of was bred there in high ceilings and in such discussions as these. Then he pitied Brendan the way he pitied himself; with that he was sitting with his head down. He was concentrating on the silence. The room was more silent than before. In the distance, the three o'clock whistle blew at the local cotton mill. In the Town of Boldface, hundreds of people were getting off work, having done jobs which, Owen supposed, had kept them in dignity. He fancied himself doing such jobs. Times he watched, being downtown for a pair of shoes or a dental appointment, the women who came from the mill. Their bodies were shapeless, and they wore mismatched colors and pedal-pushers. Their hair fell with sweat and one invariably could see the concentric rings of perspiration gathered at their armpits. He was repulsed.

He touched underneath his own arm. He felt his own sweat, noting also with repulsion the white salt stains formed there. Part of every morning for the past ten years he had got up ahead of time to take a wet rag to them. He was aware that this must have been the first morning that he hadn't done so. The instant dignity of his priesthood suffered, for one thing.

52

He smelled himself, the odor like decaying milk. At the tips of his fingers the liquid turned brown in mixture with the black dye in his habit.

Now it seemed convenient to think of starting over. His models would have been St. Francis or St. Anthony, had they really ever existed.

He wanted at least to talk about it, and Father Brendan was on his mind again. The acceptable laziness made it only a moment's wish that Brendan might have helped. Owen laughed to think of himself as repentant then.

At the door, old and deaf Father Cyril Drewe was stumbling past the fleeing priest. He stopped Owen with an old monk's authority and said, "That boy they were talking about today, how much Latin has he had?"

Which lightly put him off to Miss Hone's afternoon tea and the routine that he liked and didn't like. He felt slow and walked each step as if the short distance must take too much time. He valued this time for some unknown reason. And yet he fully wanted to be at Miss Hone's.

He couldn't explain that she promised a break in time itself, a break from his smallness.

The afternoon was a splendid cool now, and the deep sun reminded him of former times when he came here as a novice on regular Sunday walks with Father Olaf Dotis. In those days they passed Miss Adelaide's house, too, but Father Olaf only said:

"She possibly knows more about the history of Boldface Abbey than anybody, any . . . uh . . . woman, that is. It's Father Affirmo who knows most."

They walked the endless perimeter road past the small

bungalow. Father Olaf carried a stick. At ease on Sunday, he wore the familiar baseball cap and his torn sweater. In the hottest weather, or the coldest. Owen then thought it refreshing that he sat with them on a stone and told them his own version of the history of their Order. He edited the news, as well, and was confused about most of what was going on, and the names and dates. He talked about "Jakes" Maritain, "Yives" Congar. Once he had given permission for the novices to watch a Christmas TV program supposed to be a salute to George Gershwin, but when Polly Bergen opened the show singing "Someone to Watch over Me," in a halter and little else, he had swished them out like an old hen, confessing that he had thought George Gershwin a hymn writer.

And so other things like that. Owen also remembered that the perimeter road, actually an access road to the Institute, used always to be strewn of a Sunday morning with the Institute students' Saturday night left-over prophylactics. Father Olaf wouldn't even look at them, then rushed the novices past the area. And Owen laughed, thinking how many times he had gone to his room after one of those walks, even then, and, well —

The sun against the air held clear. He had a dreamless image of the air lifting him up and depositing him in the field brush, as in times when he was a boy tying a counterpane at its edges and running with it in the wind. He remembered the pleasant dizziness, the dream of having wanted to do this without his clothes. Roll in the brush naked.

To his right, the field brush was golden.

And it stretched like a river down the fringe of that

54

property of which all the monks of Boldface Abbey were joint owners. It more or less divided the land as well into an inside and an outside. For that it was also the side aisle of a theater where he went for entertainment. What was his entertainment now?

SEVEN   ANNE HONE was stretching her arms out over the oxygen hose that Miss Hone had tangled around her ankles getting the tea. Now it was crumpled on the floor as well, and bound around her feet. Anne struggled with it, trying to get it loose, and enjoying the tension in this movement.

What she didn't like was the new information she had got about her aunt. They had been to the doctor for the bimonthly checkup in the afternoon. The doctor said it plainly:

"A disease called leucoplakia. She's got it here, see, in her mouth. We can go on month after month scraping out her mouth, and she could live almost indefinitely; I mean, you know your age, Miss Addie, but death is around the corner."

"Well, I'll have no part in the delay of an overdue journey to the other side, ha, ha, but I'm going to have my fun fretting," said Miss Hone immediately.

Anne knew she meant this in a way that was, for her own thoughts, virtuous as well. She looked at her aunt affectionately, the "information" growing like a headache, but pushed aside by the comedy of Miss Hone's gasping, and her annoyed lower lip. She hadn't got the hose loose either, and Miss Hone wasn't cooperating beyond the point at which she, herself, acknowledged the trap. She threw the apparatus on the floor. She kept on the mask for laughs.

And Anne drew back to the wicker porch chair, looking at this mask and at Miss Hone's mime.

It wasn't anything new for her to be facing both the affection which she especially felt on these occasions, or the remorse that had to be a part of it. She had been there for almost four years now, each year expecting that this would be the last. Now she felt the delicate betrayal in the news because she had expected it so long. It was like being apprehensive in the first stages of a recovery from an ailment, then, good health restored, forgetting the disease could come back. The times she should have died and never did made the news particularly unpleasant.

Surely she had felt the matter the same way the old woman had.

Miss Adelaide had since been jollier about the words themselves. She insisted on getting out the encyclopedia on the matter, too, and she looked at all the pictures.

"I'm not much on the big C. What a way. Look at this, Annie. Lord knows I'd rather it had been my heart. Wouldn't you rather?"

She had asked the doctor specifics, and there weren't any more than he had said.

"Well, as long as we keep scraping out your mouth."

Anne said, "Oh Aunt Addie." She kept up the interior fear. Miss Hone easily forbade any serious talk otherwise. She laughed now to think that the silly hose had also turned against her.

"Well, I tell you one thing; I'm still vulnerable, but I won't let myself get bedsores." She went on, as well, talking about the Boldface monks who had died of it. She identified with them.

"God, I hope it's not going to be like that stupid Father Nimrod Becker's going butt first. Promise me you won't have my bowels sewed shut."

Anne laughed at that, reminding her that the disease was in her mouth.

She smiled, regarding Miss Adelaide with further admiration, being now, as always, ready to indulge any of the pretenses. She meant the gratitude showing in her eyes, never had been able to tell her aunt of the gratitude she felt simply for the old woman's presence. She recalled the first days when she arrived to take care of her. She did it as a lark, though it had partly been at the insistence of Miss Adelaide herself, who bluntly said, "You've had your studies abroad; you're finished with that and you're the last of the Hones. The last who'll endure me, ha, ha. You don't want them to put me in a home."

Anne barely knew her aunt in those days. She visited only occasionally with her father, the only brother of the two Hone women; she was told of their considerable privacy, and she knew that they had hush-hush conversations about her future. They had convinced her father that she needed to get away, she needed those special refinements that travel gets; she must read, as Miss Hone had always put it (standing at her desk in a white chiffon dress out of the 20s), "so that she can properly read the masterpieces. We don't want the child to be a nun."

And so both of Anne's parents had died in the meantime, her father always mysteriously silent in taking Miss Adelaide's orders, her mother less than subtle in her capitulation. She had done what they said without regret, too, and when the call came she hadn't minded. Anne kept her coolness; what she didn't say about her European education was what also kept her from worrying. She thought that perhaps she finally accepted the facts about her aunt's new troubles. What came out with present importance was Anne's fundamental awareness of the old woman's decency. What others regarded as eccentricity Anne soon learned to accept as her own model of behavior. This meant that there had once been two old-maid women, she supposed, who, as wards of the church, more particularly as wards of the first abbot of Boldface Abbey, learned devotion for that institution which sustained them. Elizabeth Hone, Anne's other aunt and Adelaide's sister, had been blind from birth, and Anne imagined with what horror both the women must have faced the problems of survival. She supposed this must have been their special luck to be cared for. Story was that from 1908, at least, they had ruled the roost, setting Boldface Abbey's entertainment precedents, for instance, having once had in José Iturbi and Madame Schumann-Heink. It was almost laughable, she imagined, that neither Miss Addie nor Miss Elizabeth had much more than a high-school education, but they had learned at least a certain elegance from the nuns who educated them at Abbot Hegel's expense. What emerged, of course, was Miss Adelaide's strange pronunciation of the names of the famous. She talked of Motezarty, Rackmaneenopf, Batch, though her favorite was Gerschtwin. But with only this she had managed to domesticate Abbot Hegel. There was no one to think ahead, she said. That was her primary virtue and so the Hone sisters had got carte blanche.

In those days, Abbot Hegel entertained lavishly too; his dinners, his parades, the regular celebrations, history had it, showed almost none of the struggles for financial survival that really bothered the abbey. And so, the prince's fame shot all over the South, along with occasional words about the deaf and blind princesses who were always at his side. That the fame no longer existed, Anne thought, was the urgent cause of Miss Hone's eccentricity.

Well, she talked about it, too, a regular topic of conversation that Anne liked: Boldface Abbey had seen better days when the monks were truer to the old principles. Her aunt didn't define the principles, and sat in the evenings listening to the Gershwin records, looking for all the world like a dowager princess, saying, "Too bad the former abbot, I mean the *real* abbot of Boldface Abbey, died. Too bad, damn it, that there's a Miss Nancy on that throne."

Her eyes sparkled when she spoke of Alcuin Hegel, and it was Anne's pleasure, she felt, to invite that response. If not to console her at the depths of her old-age laments (these weren't really that frequent) or merely to laugh at the charm with which even the deep Georgia accent seemed to put her in profound communication with history.

Funniest of all: Anne often read the poems of her dead Aunt Elizabeth since Miss Adelaide had framed them all and kept them on the walls all over the house. There were at least six hundred of them, all framed. They were the family's best link with the past. Miss Hone could recite them from memory, though she always said, "Of course I know that they're terrible poems.

If nature permitted us to be
under God's nose and not His knee,
we'd always confuse *kind* with *degree*
And God's aegis would be His apogee."

But then the delight in memory, the sad sad penance of having to let it go. Now Miss Hone's eyes were deep loving eyes, perfectly deserving of Anne's great concern. So she had stayed.

She sat opposite Miss Hone still; they laughed loudly before tackling the hose again. Miss Hone didn't really need it that much; she *liked* it. She liked the way it annoyed her critics, too, those monks who disliked her behavior in church.

Except, of course, Owen Cline, who by this time had arrived at the door and rushed to the porch quickly to help get the hose up and untangled and back into its little plastic resting place at the bottom of two nozzles at the end of the oxygen mask.

"Thank goodness you're here," Anne said.

Her eyes darted as they finally got the cord onto the floor and untangled. He held the cord with her.

Then Miss Hone insisted on getting more tea herself. They followed her in and out of the kitchen, straddling the hose. The old lady was more than gracious, though she had never done anything by the book. It was Owen's turn to remember what he had first liked about her — remembering that when they first met he was the waiter in the abbot's special dining room, which she had originally decorated and where she was then being entertained, except that Abbot Wilfrid, in those days, had the habit of making the crystal sing when the meal was over and she had to sit there and do what he wished and make the crystal sing too. Miss Hone had called him a silly fool.

61

Those days when Owen first started dropping by, she played her games to the hilt, and she winked as if to suggest that the longer they knew one another the more she would reveal her motives. Now he knew they *were* simple motives: she liked him almost alone among the many monks.

"Because you're the most vulnerable," she said, winking. "Is there anything you need? Now you tell me if there's anything you need at all." Almost every time he was there she gave him five dollars, loving to have him embrace her in payment.

She admitted that it was for the embrace. She would wait for it.

Now he saw that she was more than usually worn. He noticed, for example, that she hadn't fixed her hair. He wasn't reading exactly.

She first insisted on talking about Abbot Giles.

"And furthermore, I'm not too big on him or any of his schemes. Do *you* think I ought to give him the money he wants. You know he only wants money."

"Well, Miss Adelaide, it's not exactly that . . ."

"The hell you say. I know my monks . . ."

She fingered her cup sideways.

"The monastery door swings open; the door swings closed. I've seen them wind up in jail. They run off to South Carolina. They are vulnerable. You see, don't you, that they wouldn't be monks otherwise. Monkeys," she said. She laughed, having the mysterious grin that she always had when she talked carefully about the monastery.

"Ha, ha, here is the Adelaide Hone Memorial List of Monastic Ailments: cruelty, severity, indiscretion, vulnerability . . ."

He didn't ever know exactly what she meant, or where it came from. But he laughed. She wanted this.

"I remember the days of Abbot Hegel. *There* was a complete man; should never have been a monk. I saw him once in his drawers, ha, ha. In his drawers, did I ever tell you that?"

She shook her head in a still more distant wistfulness. She sipped her tea and stared at Anne. Owen saw in her again those charms which somehow displaced his smallness. He imagined not ever learning the truth about her. Fussing over her oxygen hose, her hearing aid, playing with Filch, she seemed to apply the same sane intensity that in church made her seem eccentric. This was a paradox. He was amused to think that her treatment of Abbot Giles might have been a defense against the very omniscience involved. He thought that perhaps she hid herself by taking the cynic's role in almost everything but her devotion to the abbey. Owen then supposed that she, knowing that, had by now also figured him out.

"They think I'm old and flooey."

"Oh now, Miss Hone."

"Well, they do. That twitty abbot. What is it with that twitty abbot?"

"Abbot Giles is having a hard time of it. Abbot Giles isn't much of a leader. He's confused."

"On his high horse."

"I wouldn't say that."

Now her soiled hands kept their movements subdued. She was growing more pensive though taking the tea steadily until she saw that this had made Owen silent too. She looked at him without speaking as she had learned to do when he was in one of his moods. This time she also looked at Anne, however. Who was still in the rocker, leaning forward on her elbow, her legs straight down. Miss Hone said, "Excuse me while I get some more tea. You two talk."

Well, if ever the time had come! She was still sitting with her arm that way, and shifted now to the right, looking at him. Her eyes were casual, though he still thought her distant. And what was she thinking but that now it might be important for her to tell him about Miss Addie's condition. Except that now, also, Owen had that look that made her not want to talk openly to him; as though, if she did talk to him, he would have too thoroughly a proper response. How poorly she read the reasoning even in his movements.

"Aunt Addie is what you'd have to call a character." She said it stiffly.

"A character."

"I'm devoted to her. I mean that I don't know anybody finer. When I first came here, it was a lark. She needed somebody to keep house. My father was insistent. You knew that?"

"We've never talked about that."

"And it was to have lasted maybe a couple of months until she got somebody else. When Aunt Elizabeth died, she hadn't a soul. You do understand."

He nodded. "I *was* thinking about Miss Addie's being a solid character. She puts on. She knows it's a show."

He was straining to find the rest. He watched the movements which seemed significantly interior. It was a matter of embarrassment, then of the adolescence he felt. But it was the time.

"You never talk about yourself."

"Ha, ha," she said.

"But you don't."

64

"Isn't my confession enough?"

"I never listen to your confession."

"Now, Father Owen."

"Do you have to call me 'Father'?"

Her face didn't redden. He wished it would. He awkwardly fooled with his collar. He said that he thought surely Miss Hone must have left the porch for a reason. Poked up his eyebrows with a smile and widened eyes.

"Miss Hone understands . . ."

"Whatever do you mean, Father?"

He struggled for the words now and it was against time and Miss Hone's nearness.

"I mean, I've often thought that, that . . ."

She leaned forward folding her hands on her knees. She sniffed, though not with purpose.

"I've thought often that *we* should talk sometime," he said. "We ought to talk about things without Miss Hone. I mean, the two of us could . . ."

She told him that they did talk. She told him that she trusted him; she didn't believe in silly conversations. This was a silly conversation if there ever was one. "Let's talk about Aunt Addie.

"It really is true that Aunt Addie has a special kind of wisdom. She fascinated me from the beginning. I've stayed for that. The sheer skill with which she manipulates the system. It's almost as if I'd been taking lessons; as if she were my own mystic, ha, ha."

"But . . ." he said.

"You're silly," she said, "and besides there are more serious . . ."

But then Miss Hone was back. She looked at them both sheepishly, asking whether she had been out long enough.

This was what Owen thought. He took his new cup of tea. He stared at Anne as she twisted demurely in the wicker rocker, her soft green summer dress trailing like water.

Filch arrived behind Miss Hone and when she had arranged her hose, he lay, belly up, at her feet. The dog stretched his feet lankly into the air, spread-eagle. Miss Hone laughed at him.

"This dog is hot and bothered," she said. "Damned if this dog isn't in another of his trying times. Poor Filchy, alone in a household with two old maids."

Neither Owen nor Anne had ever known her to be quite that earthy. With his eyes he used it to justify what he had been saying to her; as if, perhaps, they had arrived at a new understanding. At that she thought him too pleasantly un-inhibited. She was pleased to hear the bell for Vespers drone on especially for his displeasure.

When he stood, he gave Miss Hone her accustomed kiss. She didn't offer money. She frowned and took Owen's hand, which she gingerly drew up to Anne's shoulder. She held it there until Anne had pushed it aside. They were silent, he looking the more carefully.

Anne walked with him to the screen door, opened it and held it, and she shook his hand. She didn't draw back from it as he supposed she would, though at the moment she was also crying.

"Aunt Addie is dying," she whispered. She told him the doctor's news quickly.

Which bolted to his stomach. The feeling wasn't quite of anything but a new distaste for his body, for having so stupidly misread. He was on his way to Office, to a new idea of his entrapment.

Anne was on her way back to accepting the inevitable.

EIGHT   AND NOW JOHN VINCENT DANO was on his way
from Atlanta. He was taking the scenic route, having left a
little annoyed to be off this late, knowing that Abbot Giles
would long ago have been expecting him. Vinnie was determined to relax as much as possible. He had a new resolution
which said that if a doctor can't relax, then who can. He was
usually tied up because he worried about his patients. Not so
much their ailments, but his own fear of facing them. This
was something he hadn't ever discussed with Abbot Giles,
who, of course, thought that no one was more stable and
more self-sufficient than Vinnie Dano.

And really, what Vinnie disliked even more was that he
permitted himself to understand this. It was such thoughts
and such things as his love for getting in the car alone and
just going which kept him by himself all these years. When
he was alone, as always, he thought about being alone.

He drove at the full speed limit and listened to the
radio. He was smoking a cigar with his head up high in the
air and blowing the smoke out like a coal-fed train. This was
a pleasant image of himself, he thought, though he also

moved clumsily with the song whose meter he couldn't count.

Vinnie did think himself nearly handsome, unshaven as he was; this roughness was specially right.

He was thinking of the two children he had treated before he left Atlanta. They had arrived unnecessarily, brought by hysterical mothers. One had cut his eye falling off a stoop with a stick. The other had the hiccoughs. Vinnie answered the calls as he had always done. He contained his irritation so well that neither parent had known.

His next thought had this resolution: I'm tired of thinking. I'm also tired of thinking of thinking and I won't think. He knew that he wouldn't carry that out.

Now Vinnie was sleepy, somehow chronically so, though he could never sleep when he really wanted to. He was seeing himself flippantly, which was somehow the way he often saw himself these days. It was, first of all, the abbot and this visit and the way the abbot had acted last time. Giles had been nervous and self-pitying, at the last two meetings insisting on going over every inch of their relationship as though it gave him some kind of confidence.

"You're my friend, aren't you?"

Vinnie's eyes were passing over the dashboard, the smear of sunlight on the metal refracting colors and combinations of them. He especially liked colors. He liked a painting of nothing but colors and lines. He had a houseful of such paintings and it was something he had talked about to Abbot Giles, who better liked landscapes. He said that Vinnie was becoming too modern.

"In your surgery do you also possess a twentieth-century cynicism?"

"Love of color doesn't translate into cynicism, Father Giles."

What was this of late? How suddenly the abbot paced and said how virtually insane the times had become and how virtually all the world was lost from the values of a time when, once, man better understood himself?

"At least we understand each other, don't we, Vinnie? Vinnie, my only friend. Think of how many days it's been that we've talked and understood. Vinnie, think of it."

The car went easily. There wasn't any traffic. Vinnie put out his cigar and turned up the radio. The dashboard vibrated as he watched the landscape and those patterns by which the Georgia hills piled up. He could see the bag worms on low-lying brush.

Abbot Giles was on his mind unavoidably. Vinnie didn't know what he was going to say this time. He was remembering their first meeting at the summer camp the abbot's Order ran all those years ago. Vincent Dano, the absolute best of the boy diplomats who got to the top of the ranks quickly because he had been able to entertain the other boys. He made ratlike noises under his shoes with his toes, scared them with it; and for getting them to go to sleep out of fear, he had been rewarded with a counselor's job. Not that he had ever understood in the least the strange sort of power he could have over other people. Something to do with the oblivion he had always felt. This was never anything quite completely defined, but made him seem affable, he supposed. Having a question or a point to make, he simply and always said what was on his mind. It came off as stability. It was, at any rate, what had got him through the unpleasant summer when he first met Giles Logan.

Camp counseling was the only job he could get, since he had nowhere to go. Vinnie had come south from Jersey when his mother died, though he hadn't believed that he had really done it. Just got onto a highway and hitched his way. He wasn't sentimental about this getting him to Georgia, though the process also seemed prodigal. He was the son of an actor, and his mother was lonely. He never saw Sal Dano in anything but pictures, these with him wearing costumes of one sort or the other. His mother's constant remark, with an Italian accent: "He went off to make a fortune with his face."

He had done that, but without ever returning, or caring, for his son. Not that Vinnie ever really minded, for once more it had been his precious oblivion that made him able to deal with his mother's last days. He loved her and she managed adequately on the money she made doing alteration work for a furrier. She had his concern, too, her pride in the odd jobs he did in high school, and, last, his complete devotion. He would come home and find her usually asleep. He didn't care about that until he was aware that it was more or less an escape. And she did die of it. He could see her sitting in the chair with her needle, the thick black thread poking strenuously through the heavy pelts. She didn't talk much and kept Sal Dano's picture too close for it to have been anything but sentiment. And so Vinnie came and went to do what his own simple living required. To tell the truth, he thought, she had died rather painlessly.

He lived like an otter in this remembrance, dismissing whatever surroundings reminded him that he had learned survival from distrust.

From Jersey the ride he got took him all the way, too. He convinced the people at Our Lady of Sobriety Camp of his stability, knowing little about camping and nothing at all about his family's religion. But in both, he recalled, there was an instinct that made him learn quickly. He soon wrote the horarium and became a trustee. Which came first to the attention of the priest who ran the camp and then to Father Giles Logan who was there recruiting students for Boldface Institute. Father Giles, seeing him and hearing the reports, said, "Were you to use your talents to their fullest, you could be a doctor or a lawyer; something fine."

It was his youth or his vision or his naïveté that made the advice believable. He took it, and for the years that followed seemed to get gently pushed in the right direction. He never quarreled with it, not even with the idea of being what Giles said he should be, or any of what that took. Boldface Institute gave him his biology degree. The State Medical College graduated him with honors. How had it happened?

This might have been finally the one thing Vinnie Dano didn't really understand about himself: it all seemed an incredible instant in time, and somehow outside him. Like the superficial nearness of the car dash which he could touch, of course, but which was not the substance he might have wished it to be.

He drove the car with one hand. Tooled a finger casually around the spokes in the wheel. Father Giles had always been there, he thought. His earliest help had been to get Vinnie a new start with one of the monks who hadn't liked him, who heckled him in class. Giles always got him summer work, helped him with the money situation. But always, too, at a great distance.

Father Giles was angry with him only once, and that was

when he had done a few things with a girl at the nuns' school down the road. She would do anything, this girl. When she was pregnant the nuns said that she said it was Vinnie who did it. He told Father Giles that yes, he did a few things, but not that.

Giles Logan flushed out the real offender in a week.

But it wasn't really such things as that, either.

Most of it was, in those days as now, this remoteness thing. He felt a haze come over him sometimes, and this haze controlled his eyes and put his head into a block. It was like smelling formaldehyde. He couldn't shake this haze, and he told Giles. Then it went away.

He meant to be totally grateful when he wrote the priest a letter about it, and Giles kept this letter. He still had the letter and used it as an example of success, both his and Vinnie's. When it was the least bit pertinent, the abbot read that letter in sermons even though Vinnie had asked him not to.

Accordingly, Vinnie remembered every word:

It's a feeling of being lost. It's because of summertime mostly, but then it's so much to do with the way things smell, like smelling mustard when you've got flu.

Well, we talked. You said that it was all too common for people to feel this way. People get easily lost. This is the first time I ever heard a priest say anything like that.

What I've got to say is that I didn't figure anything out, but I did keep doing what you told me, thinking of the day it would pass. For the moment, it's gone. Is that faith?

It hadn't ever passed, especially in light of its confinements. This feeling, which even the letter didn't adequately describe, kept Vinnie as distant from other people as Abbot

72

Giles seemed always to be. There had been no close associates at Boldface Institute, no one in medical school, not even a best friend. He had women friends; he enjoyed their company, to touch them, and he might have got serious with at least one of them had it not been for the halfheartedness that always skirted his affection. Love-making was only complete because Vinnie didn't say anything.

That had to mean that Giles Logan was as much his only friend as he was Giles's. For the time being this was all going sour with the abbacy. He simply wanted to put it aside because he didn't like the monks of Boldface. As for religion, it had never been the thing those men seemed only partly to serve. Vinnie hadn't ever taken them seriously, so that, finally, what he realized was that he didn't like the revelation in being the abbot's friend. For that matter, the abbot's job itself was peculiar, though he supposed men were abbots because they were best able to get above the eccentricities of their monks.

But Giles was a decent man. He really wasn't like the others. First of all, Giles had no evasiveness about him at all, but they hadn't discussed that.

Vinnie was near the abbey at last. He was more apprehensive. What, after all, would he say this time? He hadn't any sensible advice. He wanted to be detached from the situation. Finally, there was nothing else he wanted to talk about.

The signpost called Boldface Abbey a historical site: EIGHTY YEARS IN OPERATION EDUCATING YOUNG MEN IN WISDOM AND STATURE.

He was ready to stop thinking again. He narrowly felt the motion of his car turning left and facing the rural highway that stretched almost in a straight line the rest of the

73

way. This was really what students regarded as the entrance to Boldface Abbey.

He saw the figure in black next, hitchhiking. And when Vinnie was close enough he could see that the man was Father Brendan Price. He was badly drunk. His eyes were red. His hands trembled fugitively and he was moving carelessly in his black suit. He stumbled and fell backward.

Vinnie stopped the car. He got out. He said, "Father Brendan?"

Who was all but defeated in his eyes. They were sadly upward and he said, "Those damn fools." He did recognize Vincent Dano, and he said that he had to get out of there. It wasn't worth anything anymore, and what could he do, knowing about himself this way. "And Myrtis."

"Well, Father, let's get you home."

"Tut, tut, you know that I can explain this of course. Well, you see, these two thugs . . . uh, stole my car — you don't see a car — they beat me up and I'm this way because . . ."

He laughed out loud with that lie, matching his words with the bounce with which he started himself standing.

"You," he said.

And then Vinnie hadn't any reservations about it unless they were the ones on his mind a moment earlier. Not using any of his thoughts to make prescriptions, refusing it even in principle, he conned the monk into the car. They went on down the road, silent. Soon Father Brendan had breathed himself to sleep, after looking at Vinnie with complete openness. He felt comfortable leaning his head on the physician's shoulder. Which Vinnie accepted, breath and all, in the name, now, of his own search for a way to avoid talking about it.

74

NINE THE DIFFICULT PART was trying to do what Father Brendan asked and get him up the back stairs without being seen. Halfway up, they saw the monks come out onto the back porch before supper. The abbot himself appeared, and Father Affirmo, and half a dozen of the rest.

And Father Owen Cline.

Father Brendan was singing "Over the River and through the Woods" and the abbot was staring, bewildered, rushing down the steps with Vinnie's greeting in mind. He tried not to embarrass the priest and he leaned over to him and listened to him mumbling inaudible sentences with that dignity only Father Brendan could evince, even in this condition.

Brendan slapped Vinnie on the back, "We must do this again some time."

The abbot laughed, watching Vinnie and saying with his eyes the greeting that would have been customary. He did pity Brendan, but didn't want the situation to threaten the evening. He felt ashamed that they all seemed to know this perfectly well. They were all contemptuous.

And so he was silent, taking the priest's arm, Vinnie taking his other arm, Father Owen coming down to help too. The faces around were stolid, for the most part, and motionless, in contrast to the surrounding light and the dust that always rose when there was someone walking on the back porch.

Then the real interest was Owen's. He saw the drama, considering it unusually familiar. He was drawn to it as though it might have been a new facet of his now compulsory game. He managed to fight bitterness, however, pitying Father Brendan.

Whose room was strewn with papers and books, some old exams partly corrected from years back, and they put him down in his bed, which was also full of papers. They couldn't find a blanket. Now Brendan was saying, "Oh how sorry I am."

He went on, "I had to get out of here. The futility . . ." He grimaced toward each of them. "But there is a God, you know."

The abbot said, "Now, now, Father; now, now, it's not easy and we know it's not easy. Here, Father, rest awhile."

It was Father Owen who showed his compulsion to stay. The game functioned to train his look on the abbot and Vinnie Dano. All the while their faces showed immediacy. Owen said he knew that they wanted to visit and talk. He said he understood that it was their weekly chat. He said, "If you want to go on, then don't worry about it, and I'll take care of this." He helped Brendan undress down to his yellowed drawers. He covered him up in a blanket that he got from the closet in the hallway.

So that when Abbot Giles and Vinnie were gone he sat

76

and waited as if he expected a revelation. He got nothing. He only watched Brendan breathing stagnantly. He, like most of the monks at Boldface, had taught dozens of subjects over the years. He had taught Owen a course in Renaissance history. The words from that year seemed to have emerged in Owen's mind as though Brendan would have wanted them to be his concern. Owen saw him quite as he saw himself making profound statements which came out of the well-spring of their discipline, at least out of those issues which at the time had stirred his own mind to splendid belief in both the doctrine and its exercise. In those days no one of them could have escaped the force with which their wise confrere had said, "If man is immortal, we want to be outside ourselves. But, of course, there're other things besides immortality. Don't you see that we're afraid, and this means there is a God? This is what monks serve." He stood in his towering way and ground his feet into the classroom floor and the boards creaked as if they knew where he would step next. These were the days before he had started drinking. Almost everybody at one time or another went to him for advice. Even when he was drunk, on occasion, and back when confession was still a part of the regimen, the line was long outside his door on Friday nights. The penances were easy, Owen remembered. The advice was for regular bathing, readings from the church fathers, prayer for the poor souls, and for Brendan Price, God's fool.

In retrospect, Owen then thought he could imagine the day when things with Myrtis had caught up with him. He could remember them together on the perimeter road, sitting out under the oaks on the entrance avenue, she taking notes in one of her print dresses; he cautious to let them know that it was strictly business. Even when Owen first arrived at the monastery the monks had known. They had been the laughingstock of the community when Abbot Wilfrid found them in the basement amidst his movie equipment.

Then they had moved her around to save her, put her in the library to work, where Owen had noticed sadly the patient and capacious eyes, even then, adjusting to changing circumstances. How had these two survived was the question for him. How had Brendan managed to keep her near?

Which seemed then the perfect revenge against all the upsetting principles.

Owen was fingering his own wrist when the priest leaned off the edge of the pillow; his eyes went open and focused and he saw Owen. He wasn't embarrassed, nor had he done anything but look as if he were glad to have this confrere there. The faint blessing of recognition had sparked an ease for both of them.

"Of all the people to be here."

"Well, Father, I . . ."

". . . you needn't be sympathetic." This with a grunt, his hands folding as he tried to sit.

"I'm not sympathetic; I'm just here. Better me than the rest . . ."

"That's not true, son . . ."

"Well, do you want me to go?"

"No, no, don't do that. Did I make you sore? Didn't mean to. What are they saying? Are they saying 'he's at it again'?"

"Nothing, Father Brendan."

Brendan coughed and folded his hands on his chest again and stared at the ceiling without saying anything; the two of them were generally unable to find the next thing.

Brendan finally said, "I've been here for twenty-eight years. Is it hard to believe that? It's hard for me to believe that."

Owen nodded.

"And, you know, when I first came here, I had no idea that it would last."

"Well, monasticism *is* dying, Father . . ."

"You're a fool for saying that . . ."

"Look at you, Father; look at . . ."

He had no idea why he said it; he hadn't wished to hurt him. But he felt the thread of cynicism tighten again quickly. He was looking at the past and gauging his own disposition again. He thought of the chapter meeting, of Miss Hone and Anne. These were his distractions.

Until at last Brendan was watching him as though he knew all of it exactly, and as if he might want to be prophetical. He said, "But you're at the right age to say that."

"That?"

"Doubt, presumption, inconvenience."

He tightened his fists and his mouth and he struggled to sit again. He sat against the wall next to the bed, propped up on a pillow.

"What I was trying to tell them at the chapter meeting was that we're all going to die sooner or later. This is the best life for it; I mean, we have a way for preparing that nobody else has. But it's wasted in those petty . . . The life here makes it the least painful, I want to tell you. I'm certain; you shouldn't doubt it."

"Death isn't my problem," Owen said.

Brendan said, "Oh, yes it is."

And Owen listened toward the far window and heard the late Saturday Mass crowd going home. Watching Father

Brendan move back under the covers, he rubbed his chin and thought of this priest out hitchhiking as Vincent Dano had reported. What it must have been like for a man like this to have been trying to get away. One of the constant arguments for the dignity of their work was that all of them were giving up important jobs in the world to be there. He wasn't; Brendan wasn't.

But then Owen disliked himself again for that one. He heard the sounds from outside grow louder. He was thinking about his own sin; thinking that, indeed, Brendan was covering up in platitudes. Owen thought that he hadn't even any platitudes. He was thinking how little pleasure he got from it. And of the emptiness and its fear. He suddenly wanted to be as aware as possible of his surroundings. He deliberately wanted to smell the odor of Father Brendan's breath, to know the impact of the air and hold on to whatever, at the moment, seemed unexpendable.

The specter of sin and the force of the word itself, his own distrust for the word now, made him contemptuous of the sympathy he was feeling. The real problem was that none of them enjoyed their life. He wanted to *say* it to Father Brendan.

Say the Divine Office was a chore. This dry and lengthy repetition of the Psalms was finally only a mixture of platitudes as well; the only relief from the routine was the times they could laugh at Father Phineas's music, mistakes at ceremonies. This was preparation for death?

It *was* death.

He was seeing in Father Brendan less regard for the priesthood too. He still cared for him, though the lank figure was gnawing at the air and melodramatically crying, and Owen could see no one but himself.

80

Then Brendan said, "You watch that you don't start thinking yourself better than they are. I mean better in any way. This isn't a perfect world. Oh, I've done a terrible thing!"

The voice moved in the high and low points of studied rhetoric, but it was a forlorn voice.

TEN   OWEN SKIPPED MATINS and went to his room. Supper had been the usual Saturday breaded veal cutlet, and he overate. He always looked forward to meals because there was somebody to talk to. The chapter meeting was the topic of conversation, and they had all been careful to avoid talking about Brendan Price. Owen had sat with Father Affirmo and Father Phineas and didn't know why except that they made him laugh sometimes. This time they railed against Abbot Giles, noting with special pleasure that he would be absent for Matins to be with Vinnie.

"Uh, his little friend," Affirmo joked.

And it was a moment which both he and Phineas took to lament how sad, sad it was that Giles didn't get along with any of *them* that well.

"I suppose it's because we don't *like* him, ha, ha," said Affirmo.

"Or, instead, that we don't . . . uh . . . *love* him," smirked Phineas.

They laughed bitterly until Owen had found it too much. He had two strawberry tarts, the pastry dough only partly cooked and sterile. Affirmo had eaten little while Phineas plied him with his views of the chapter meeting.

That was why, finally, the thought of Matins with them had sent Owen to his room. Which meant now that if he wanted to go down and watch television, or get a snack in the community room later, he would have to explain his absence at Office. Saturday nights got more attendance than any other time.

It got more attendance in the community room as well. For one thing, the monks knew that Abbot Giles would be with Vinnie Dano. The eleven o'clock curfew would be relaxed; at least there would be no scene over those who defied him and watched the late show.

Owen found all this distasteful of course. He thought of Miss Hone as the only person he would even care to talk to anymore. He thought of going back down there, maybe even to comfort the old woman. He wanted to. And to see Anne Hone.

But it left him only with what he supposed would go on happening; this time it must get him to sleep. He most dreaded the nighttime and, waking up with nothing to do, he would force himself to lie there horrified by the silence. There *was*, in fact, nothing to do. Even when school was in session, he didn't like the so-called teaching he did in the college because it was repetitive; the clubs he moderated, the students he saw, came and went without lasting as though they were somehow tokens of the unending boredom. They came back to visit when they had children and wives, always expecting to be remembered. This, again, was the priesthood.

Now it was time for him to remember with what admiration he had first come here. It was routine that he first remembered his earliest interest not to have been with the life at all; it was the uniform. He imagined that this was true of all of them, that lure of dignity that the habit offered falsely, and all the thousands of ways one protected oneself with it. He had liked the black flowing lines. The years had so fitted him to the skirt that he found himself embarrassed when he climbed public stairways in street clothes and reached automatically to pick up his cassock. He found it all in a vocations' book where the habits of each Order were represented. Most of the outfits, except for the very ancient, were laughable, as with one contemplative group that advertised its religious in long Renaissance cloaks, wearing crowns of thorns, beside a golden crucifix: BEAR YOUR CROSS FOR CHRIST, it said. That picture he had saved in the interests of teaching introductory sociology. Owen didn't really have one subject that he taught more than a year at a time.

He came to the monastery suspecting that interests and reservations such as these would finally dismiss the monastic life itself; teaching, it now seemed, promised a large measure of that dignity he also saw in the monastic garb. But that turned sour in the prescriptions the Order used. All of them had taught everything from mathematics to cake decorating, and what about all the initial promises where on his recruitment visit he had talked with Abbot Wilfrid and Wilfrid said that the world is a collection of unseen dignities? It was for monks to bring such things to the surface. What a spectacular theory that had been for an eighteen-year-old, but he could never remember its doing anything but complementing his misshaped interest in people, thriving, worse, on statistics and obviation.

84

Now it was an unquestionable limbo. He felt himself incapable of colorful theories. He thought about Miss Hone, trying to generate sympathy again. He wasn't compelled beyond indifference.

Prayers? He remembered the suggestions of Father Olaf Dotis from faraway too: Lord help my unbelief. Then Father Brendan on evil.

"God in heaven, do something with my evil."

This went quickly, almost comically as Owen turned in his bed. The bed was too warm. He thought he must do something. Get up. Sit. Talk further to himself.

The partial light from his shaded window was coming in slants against the mirror across the room. Now came ambivalence as he counted the slants of light. He could trace the evolution of his detachment, the earliest moments of his Profession when he fully accepted the burden of being a protector of the truth which the church thought essential to man's salvation. Yet he had preached it always under the cloud of superficial unworthiness; like any priest who spoke with authority, he was forced to see himself outside the framework of the system he would have praised. He still spoke of himself, however; the sermons which proclaimed that the church must be obeyed had meant that *he* must be obeyed.

He roundly talked of faith in those days, and went out to preach it with a faddist's spirit. He seriously believed the church's great truth, though in the name of his own weakness he found it patronizing.

The next stage had seen faith, if he dared call it that anymore, slip to a kind of theatricality where he still mouthed the words and preached the sermons but found them useless. The lights on the wall counted those times as well, and moments when he had almost been forced to cry out against the deception.

Then this limbo. He wanted to blame somebody for it at last. The groaning coming from far down inside him and making him turn without comfort now seemed willing to rage at everybody, even Anne Hone.

Then the colorless blanket of self-knowledge, of this degeneracy, of faithlessness, fell like his own rhetoric into pretense.

The slants of light danced to his groans; no, to his sighs, and to the restoration of those moments when the pain made it all clear. He was a child, and he would never grow up. Now the reflections were a checkerboard. He rubbed his face, his neck and shoulders, trying for some momentary nirvana. If he could only be limp and completely aware of the impulses of his body. If he could relax to the point of only feeling, not thinking, not preaching to himself. He was then assuaged by the possibilities in it — you get to a point where you merely see yourself in connection with other objects, you are a part of them, you feel their existence, and you find peace.

He traced his hands slowly over his face again; he felt the thickness of his eyebrows and drew them out in little strands, suddenly aware of their length; he touched easily the small blemishes on his skin, the deepened soft tarn in his gullet, the symmetry of his collar bones. He took hold of the fabric of his undershirt, carefully rubbing it and then pressing it against his chest where he listened to the current against the hair. It wasn't as usual; he felt no compulsion to be stimulated.

The rhythms of the moonlight had continued quite in contrast to his own slow movements, and at last he could hear the patterns developing like the tick of a clock. He had wanted to hear an almost three-quarters time beat, but gave in warmly to the natural pattern.

Now it was all transferred to his sense of smell, the thick granular odor of what had to be the final token of this new awareness. The light pleasure of it, the near sleep, and at last the kind madness of being able to let himself go in the spark of the moment. He touched himself with still further warmth. He was resting, possessing a light, helping himself to the orgasm that finally rested at the edges of a metaphorical silence. He heard Father Brendan Price: death is what troubles you.

Now it almost meant salvation. He hadn't thought of its being the third time. He hadn't thought of the abuse itself, the soreness of an overspent body. This only gave to him, in proportion to the fear which sustained him, a punishment, maybe, and then a moment of futility.

So he turned over in the semen, crying.

ELEVEN   LAUGHING, Abbot Giles and Vincent Dano had dismissed the scene with Father Brendan for the moment, and Owen. They went quickly to the abbot's room where Giles had already got a fifth of bourbon and an ice bucket. He was prepared to skip supper and Vespers for this. He had written out the formulas for Abbot Wilfrid to take his place.

In the chapel the monks noted his absence, among them, Father Affirmo, who had the reading that evening, and stood in his stall, leaning against the back rail; he contemplated walking out of the Service in protest.

He caught Father Phineas's eye as the latter plumped the music on the organ rack; and he nodded to the abbot's vacant place; then toward Abbot Wilfrid who fidgeted and played around with the papers. He moved his glasses up and down on his face because he had never learned to be comfortable with bifocals. He also had a kind of dyslexia. This would, as when he had the abbacy, stretch the ceremony by fifteen minutes.

This was what Father Affirmo alluded to with a deep, deep sigh.

Abbot Wilfrid did let the bell go, and the voices, uncompellingly chanting "Oh, Lord, come to my assistance," had gone up through the garden and to the second-floor abbot's quarters where the abbot and Vinnie could hear them. They were heard for their sluggishness, of course, but far more for their fewness in number.

The abbot was standing by his window and listening and he resisted getting the conversation off to a bad start with this. He lifted his glass loftily.

He said, "Well here's to the next thousand years."

Vinnie was in the room's only easy chair. He was rubbing his eyes with his free hand, looking with a sigh and his usual uncalculating demeanor.

"Ha, ha, ha. You really do believe in that stuff. I mean you really do go out there and say prayers and you really do think that you are some kind of a Christ to them."

So it was off to a bad start anyhow since it was the first time Vinnie had ever said anything like that. And the first time it hadn't been up to the abbot to find the subject.

"What about Father Brendan?" Vinnie said.

"Do we have to talk about that?" Giles asked. "I want to show you something," he continued, and he went over and opened the desk drawer and took out the monastery plans and held them up.

"Finished," he said. "Do you think they'll ever like that?"

Vinnie said, "What I want to know is whether you ever think about anything important!"

Giles cleared his throat. This had hurt him. It was even

89

less the proper way to begin the evening. Then it was a matter of trying to find a better way.

"Vinnie, you are my only friend, and . . ."

"Please don't start that stuff again; I mean please don't really."

What came to Giles's mind was the disposition that Vinnie usually had. He thought of his being here as before, quietly listening to him, of Vinnie's speech which recalled his indebtedness to the abbot.

Vinnie's formerly engaging smile was wilted and he was distant. Nor was he looking at Giles. He was looking into his glass, stirring the ice.

"Then something must be wrong, Vin?"

The room was darkening with the dusk. They hadn't put on the lights and from outside Vespers was still coming up, heightened by the addition of Father Harold who could always be heard because of his special enunciation of the word "Lord."

Vinnie and the abbot sat quietly then. There were fresh smells of the evening.

"You know," Vinnie said, "but I really don't suppose you *do* know, that I'm tired of my medical practice. I'm resentful of people with stupid ailments. This morning I had two children with silly mothers. *My* mother had stupid ailments."

In effect, Abbot Giles was noticeably pleased to have the silence broken. He hadn't really heard what Vinnie said. He had only got the tenor of it. It was like former days when Vinnie came to him with problems.

Vinnie said, "I really am tired of what I do. The old answers are bad now." He was thinking in particular of the feelings he had had coming down in the car.

Vinnie was recalling the only other incident in his life when he had felt like running. It was the whole business that had brought him where he was. He remembered his mother sitting at the table in the kitchen in the last days; she was eating cereal which, in those days, was her only food because she didn't feel, as she said, like eating anything else. Her face was sordid, then, in its deathly paleness, though the life fought to surface. It was the days, he recalled, when she finally gave up all claim to him and told him he ought to go off and leave her. He had asked how he could do that, and she, more with intended humor than with doom, said, "As well you as your father; then I will have lost both my men." Vinnie did love her immeasurably. She brought out the photographs of Sal Dano, his striking face, mustachioed dark mouth, like Vinnie's. It had a subtle grin. It signified the dependency he had for her.

This was what finally troubled him now, and he looked on Giles's broodings with some reservation. Might he, thus, be deepening the same kind of dependency? The word itself troubled him. He thought of having no friends but Giles; the year brought those good moments between them, almost as if, somehow, Giles adequately played all the parts of a best friend. They *had* talked. Best, Giles supported him in the personal routines he couldn't explain. He had told Giles that it pleased him to go to the office in the daytime, pushing the sad oblivion he felt into spectacular service. He laughed when he had to, joked with two nurses and the receptionist without actually knowing them. All sorts of people preferred his calm, the steadiness of his hands, and his nonchalance. Who were his friends but the receptionist, the nurses with whom he was businesslike? The faceless women, too, whom he approached only in extreme need.

Home was his joy. Giles had encouraged him to buy an eighteenth-century farmhouse which he fixed up: he selected the furniture, planned the colors; he painted the house, supervised the accessories even; and went there happily in the evenings to sit, have his drink, listen to some music, read himself to sleep.

Had it been Giles who also did this to him? Certainly it was what the abbot had led him to. He couldn't fathom the loyalty. He couldn't fathom at all the strange contentment of it. He held his face rigidly in this, a prolonged smile, like the silence.

Then Vinnie at least disliked the trivial aspects of these thoughts. He diluted the inconsistency with an awareness that his drink was taking hold. He wanted, really, to be elsewhere.

So that Giles, on the other hand, stared at the ceiling. He listened to the ice sounding like a wind chime. He felt his sensibilities giving way. He had no real sense of Vinnie's presence for a time; the feeling being a desire to be up somewhere away where he wasn't caught by time and space. For this it didn't matter that he was an abbot, or a religious, or anything. For this he didn't even need to think of God, let alone put himself in the position of speaking for God. His doubt collected all the moments of adjustment that he had made in his journal where he admitted a reprehensible self. He was tired.

He thought again of himself in the days when he had first been elected and how he had stood before the mirror in the new red cassock, rochet carefully draped. He tried on the zuchetto and positioned it many times for the fit as he did all too often these days. Ultimately it was as unbecoming as anything else he wore. He didn't want to wear anything.

92

There was something coming from the distance like the lights again, and calling. Now he only looked in his easy admission of tiredness.

Abbot Giles thought that what he really always protected Vinnie from was running away too. This was where one needed formulas. There was the time Vinnie decided that school was a bore, that being in the South was a dismal business. And he might as well pack up and go back to Jersey where at least it wasn't so hot. Then he spoke of being tired, and seeing nothing in the studies but a bewilderment. He would prefer, he said, to be out in the sun, or he would prefer at least being somewhere distant and changeless. Here he locked his head into that famous haze again, not knowing spring from summer, or winter from fall. The seasons and time, study, the place, weren't exotic enough.

Giles just told him that this kind of thing worked inward, touched too completely on the problem of human folly. "The Greeks called it *akedia*. We don't give in to it because it would break us loose from the world. The world has to stay what it is. It's just that we're stuck with the world!"

Giles, of course, regarded this as pretentious now. The distinctions were there as if he were still, himself, twenty-three and first tasting the glories of counseling. Both monasticism and his own remoteness worked it away intolerably. These were, if anything, the traditional apologetical lines that the church stood by for eternity. But Giles was saying to himself that there really was no lasting way to tell *anybody* that life was only what it was without being silly. He no longer thought he believed this either.

There he was deploring the thought, while they both had the rest of their drinks and talked about the monastery

93

plans. Vinnie finally agreed that it was in the interests of the community. He joined Abbot Giles, sat in the abbot's chair. Vinnie smiled boyishly and leaned back. He put on the abbot's zuchetto and rapped on the desk.

"OK now, all you complaining sons of bitches and all you peeing, groaning deaf and dumb old fools; hear me for I *am* your abbot."

"Ha, ha, ha."

"I *am* your abbot and here is what I say: I say give up your alien ways and come unto me . . ."

His arms had gone forward like an orchestra conductor, the muscular body moving downward in the chair. Vinnie swung around and around.

The abbot watched intently. He was suddenly aware of the physical Vinnie as though he had never paid any attention to it. These were dark, hirsute arms. Vinnie's stub of a neck slid athletically down to a pair of severe shoulders. The open collar of a nylon shirt showed still more hair.

The abbot turned quickly. There were frightening specters of his remoteness again and his long-practiced distance from Vinnie. Yet there was a longing whose forces he didn't understand. He feared the touches of other people, having dreaded the moments in his ordination when the bishop put his hands on his head or traced his fingers with Holy Oils. So also the ritual of the Pax. Nor had he ever been close to anyone, even to Vinnie when, during all the years, he had listened to his childlike personal confessions. By ritual, he remained on the other side of the room.

Now it seemed that he hadn't ever known John Vincent Dano at all, or anybody else. He was tired of the day, of his two years in producing formulas. He was absorbed in the thought that he really couldn't feel the nearness of anybody or anything. But he was aware that today had been different. What of the sudden feelings for his clothing? His lights?

Abbot Giles went quickly to the other side of the room. He looked at Vinnie from there, while Vinnie went on with his mockery. Then Vinnie was sitting quite still.

He said, "What's wrong with *you*?"

The abbot sipped his drink.

"Nothing."

"You look pale as a ghost."

The abbot stroked the chain of his pectoral cross. He moved closer. He was feeling space going wild and feeling conviction and strength. He moved next to Vinnie and put his hand on his shoulder.

He said nothing, forced to see Vinnie drawing back. Vinnie looked at the abbot calmly, however. He thought of the darkness and somehow of the emotion which confused both of them. He took Giles's hand strongly and shook it.

Neither was superficial in this, but there was a difference in their appraisals of one another. They didn't speak.

Abbot Giles held on. The primitive quality of the release forced this.

Yet he felt a change, and Vinnie did, and while they spent the rest of the evening stumbling to get back to old times, and talking around them, their minds kept trailing off, moment to moment, toward the distance to which each wished a return, but which neither had the formula for regenerating.

TWELVE   So WAKING EARLIER than usual the next morning, the abbot prayed. He wrote what he was thinking
quickly in his journal, sitting at the desk in his pajamas:

> I am secretly going to write that there aren't any formulas;
> there shouldn't be, and here, Lord, you must understand
> that I am led even further to dismiss the hope that your house
> will be what the rules have wanted. Not *this* house.

He was up and off to the Morning Office, to Lauds with
its particularly heavy ritual. Lauds was three Psalms, a reading, which by now they had heard hundreds of times, a single
prayer: Lord, allow us to accept the day according to precept.

The sacristan was at the back of the chapel, startled that
the abbot had arrived earlier than usual, but beaming as well
with an old man's excitement at what he had to tell.

"There's a woman out there," he began, and moved
closer to the abbot to whisper, "who is lying on the altar with
her face up. She came in when I opened up this morning.
She came in and got up on the altar. The woman is
deranged."

The abbot went quickly to look, and she lay with her hands to the ceiling, legs stretched together, face up on the main altar looking like a corpse. She was mumbling: "Sixty-four, twenty-three, thirty-eight, a hundred and two."

And then the monks began to arrive and the news traveled fast. Father James, who rarely if ever made it to Lauds, asked, "Who is she?"

"Nobody knows, but she's different from the one last year who took off her clothes in the narthex."

They had all begun to laugh, congregating near the back door and going and coming with the excitement.

"Well, what shall we do?" asked the sacristan. "We can't carry on Lauds with a deranged woman on the altar."

"We must try to get her off," the abbot said. "We must be kind to this woman, and we must try to reason with her."

"Is this woman dangerous?" asked Father Affirmo, stepping from the back, holding the Book and tapping it nonchalantly.

The abbot went out to the woman. Her face was pale, though worn. She was a mill woman, her hands scarred. She had long and shaggy hair, and wore brown trousers with grease on them. She refused to speak but for her incantations. The abbot touched her arm and she was unflinching; the heavy glaze in her eyes didn't allow her to seem aware of where she was.

"Can I do anything to help?" Giles said, but she continued to do what she was doing. He recognized his own deliberation. He reviewed the prescriptions of the psychology manuals he knew while the monks came, one by one, to try their own particular approaches.

There was Affirmo abruptly taking her stiffened arm and

trying to pull it forward so that she would sit up. She wouldn't, and she was too heavy for him to lift.

Father Olaf Dotis bent over her quietly, saying, "My dear young woman, this is a Catholic church and we're particularly cautious as to the sacredness of our altars. I would think that simple courtesy ought to demand that you remove yourself from here."

Father Dorian: Where is your husband, madam?

Father Phineas: Come now, dear lady, we're monks and we understand how difficult the world is.

Father James: Perhaps, madam, if we prayed together . . .

Came Father Conrad with his cool approach. He sauntered by as if not to notice, lifting his hand in a little wave, "Oh hello, how are you today?"

Then half a dozen more until the woman began to scream her numbers more wildly and stretch out her arms. She hit two of the monks.

"The police," said Affirmo, standing with his book. "We might hurt her; she might hurt herself."

They did call the police and stood back now, each in an auxiliary enterprise either of prayer or pity, some, still, of laughter.

The abbot stood particularly at attention, without saying anything, feeling the cries of the woman somewhat soothing; his own instincts operated out of the vibrations of her voice as a wild impulse. He identified with this.

They went on with Lauds elsewhere, but the abbot stayed behind with Affirmo and the sacristan, watching her. They sent for Vinnie who came down in his pajamas and told them that they had done the right thing in sending for

98

the police. He stood lazily next to the altar and took the woman's frantic pulse. He looked at the abbot cautiously then, as though he had expected their first eye contact to be particularly difficult. It was.

Abbot Giles looked helpless to him, and Vinnie, himself, wasn't really able to sleep. Through the night he dreamed of simply getting in his car and going again. This time he was sustained by the reveries of motion. The abbot was also on his mind.

The police came, six men in lazy uniforms of the sort that only Southern policemen wear; they were dressed shabbily as if they might, instead, have been janitors.

They were more concerned with the way the abbot and Vinnie looked than with the woman. In the cavernous church they waddled forward eerily, whispering to themselves, and unable to draw their lips seriously together.

The abbot told them that here was, somehow, a deranged poor soul that they didn't know what to do with.

"Did she get up there huhself?"

"What —? Do you think we put her there?"

"Well, uh, Cath'lics is a kind of superstition 'round here, suh. I mean don't get me wrong nor nothin' like that."

"The woman came into church this morning when it was opened. She came in, apparently, to pray, but there she is on the altar. Now what are you going to do about it?"

"Yeah, yeah, yeah."

This lead officer approached the woman as if he were about to raid a still.

He gave the other men an ample nod, and they came over and stood around the altar. They stared until the woman herself had seemed to come out of her daze. Seeing

99

the police, she began to cry and scream that at last her army had arrived. It was truly Armageddon, she said, and she, the Queen of Sheba resurrected, would lead them to protect God's chosen 144,000.

"Sixty-two over there in Judah, twenty-three for the Tribe of Benjamin, thirty-eight for Reuben, a hundred and two for Asher . . ."

She ran from officer to officer; she dubbed them knights and lords, princes, and all along grew happier and happier until she could barely contain it.

"This here's a job for the Rescue Squad," the lead officer said, and he added, "Or else this is some special brand of Cath'lics, ain't it? Ain't it the Cath'lics which has princes and kings and what-not?"

He said to the abbot, "Yes this is for the Rescue Squad and I'll call; or, mistah, you'd best maybe take care of your own."

Then the abbot was neither baffled nor resigned. He knew the rural mind and he, at last, didn't care as he watched the woman romp through the church letting herself go wildly. The abbot's own lights were in operation. He might have felt compelled to join her. It was Father Affirmo, goading him with the possibilities of scandal, who got him at last to take the woman's purse and look for an identification.

They found her name and the Rescue Squad came and they sent for her daughter, who, dressed like her mother, came reluctantly. Both women left on the arms of officers of the Rescue Squad, though the deranged one looked back in special pity.

Father Affirmo and the abbot and Vinnie Dano simultaneously recognized the unwarranted clumsiness of their concern. They were silent, and the abbot cast an especially grim look toward Vinnie. Who said he was going back to bed.

The church was quiet with its special flavor of morning ebullience; light coming through the most worn parts of the stained-glass windows and, comically, most clearly through the knee of the figure of Saint Bernard, whose pose was supposed to have been famous. The immense vaulted ceiling, as in the monastery, was tin, making the building appear much larger than it was. The builder had been a ship's carpenter from the old days. The nave of the church *was,* in fact, a nave, having all the angles and ridges of an upside-down ship. When Giles had first come there he had gone up into the rafters which were thinly hidden by the sheets of tin filigree. And there found the names of hundreds of Boldface Abbey students carved in profusion. He found graffiti concerning Abbot Hegel, always complimentary.

Somehow what the deranged woman proclaimed was once more fitting.

It put him back into his feelings for the past, of monks with stone constitutions, weighing their bread, retiring at ten, rising at four, chanting the psalmody in a sacrosanct form as though they were elements of feudal societies. Princes, all of them, with the finest sensibilities.

Giles sat alone in his stall, then, the lights gone, Lauds done inside. The others were at breakfast now. He was reading the Office, making it up. No, he wasn't *reading* the Office at all; he was *mouthing* it. Now he was constrained to talk about himself. He wanted to. What were these clouded elements of his feelings? Here, as before, Father Brendan seemed the only recourse. He might have been the only one to understand.

101

Father Owen Cline had come in awkwardly at this moment. He hadn't been breathless or worried, though in a circumspect way he had announced to the abbot that he had just come from checking on Father Brendan.

"He's up there dead," Owen said. "I think it must have been a heart attack in his sleep. Abbot Wilfrid's with him and Dr. Dano. An ambulance's coming. I don't know . . ."

But Giles refused to be overwhelmed. The light trailing of his thought was of Brendan's death being inevitable. Though here he wanted to cry, he kept his hands and his head from moving, and he prayed.

They went to Brendan's room where Vinnie shook his head stolidly. Abbot Wilfrid was doing the last rites while the monks in the hall sang the "Ultima."

Father Affirmo was crying far more than anyone, and he rushed to the sacristy to start the death bell.

THIRTEEN   WHICH WAS on an old-style fuse switch in the sacristy with a naked wire stretching from the top of the box through a hole in the wall and up to the carillon in the room where the organ blower was. It had been put in that way by a priest, now dead, who was also an electrician.

The speaker for the bell was in the left tower of the chapel and it blared out over the countryside, falling on the ears of the passing Methodists who didn't know what it meant; they didn't care what it meant, but sometimes in curiosity or in anger somebody would come by and ask who was sitting on it.

So the bell, besides signifying that a monk of Boldface Abbey was dead (prescription held that it must go for an hour), was the sort of curiosity that enlivened and mystified.

Father Owen was thinking all this. He was thinking it coldly, leaving the dead man's room, passing through the crowd of monks outside the hall who had, according to tradition, already begun to carry Father Brendan's belongings out into the hallway. They would put them on the windowsill and then take their choice.

He couldn't help remembering the talk with Brendan. It brought the morning on like an illusion, sustained it as stage properties perfect for his feelings; the sun cast boxlike shadows off the sides of the buildings, crosses adorning the tops perching in rigid final pronouncements, their tin underpinnings rocked by landing birds. Boldface seemed a fortress at times such as these and a perfectly insular pocket in the world of forgotten ceremonies. He lamented, was lamenting when Myrtis Crawford appeared coming up the avenue in front of him. She frantically asked was it true, eyes going wide, the fullness of her mouth stretching fiercely over teeth she didn't want to show. He watched her face drop when he nodded, not knowing exactly that she *was* there, that the situation *was* real; agreeing with her then that it was a trap that she wouldn't be able to get in there. She was stone with this realization.

"They won't let me in, will they? Women aren't allowed. Father . . . what . . ."

It made him take her arm firmly. He pushed up the defiance that might only have been at the base of his feelings, and there was a violence which almost made him laugh. She breathed freshly, in tune with him as they rushed the darkened corridors right through the cloister entrance. He excitedly counted her steps as well, seeing her hesitate only for a brief moment before she had pulled up her collar, pushed back her tears and the running mascara.

When they approached the room, Owen felt proud of her, and a certain childishness motivated him, as though it were an act of revenge, to ask the monks there to step aside.

Which they did with harsh silence, horrified.

And with that, Owen was thinking that she behaved

104

spectacularly; she rushed to the corpse which they were about to take downstairs to the ambulance. She sat next to him on the bed and stared quietly. She didn't cry now, but breathed again as if to betoken the further decision she made. While they stood around she touched his chest, not kissing him; her hands just at the bottom of his collar bone. There was a little smile, finally, when she turned back to her observers, to whom she already had begun to whisper that they needn't worry, she was going, she said, and, "Thank you. Excuse the intrusion."

They stood back without saying a word; it was that awesome, and the impact startled Owen. He might have felt even triumphant had he wished to give himself credit for the scene. But the epiphany was of a far more undefined specter, his own sudden fear that even his moment of breaking through the system hadn't meant all that much. So what that he had seen them baffled? Did it mean that he was any different from before?

He had once been impressed that when a monk died he was suddenly a monument to a tradition of survival; every year they went to the cemetery to celebrate that survival. The month was set aside for these men.

Suddenly the cynicism was full-blown. These men!

He remembered then his first day in the monastery. They sent him to serve the mass of Father Stanislaus Winter, since dead, who had an alcohol problem like Brendan's. But he had got farther with it and was disagreeable to the point of making it his pastime. He came down shaking, and stood shaking all through the consecration. And when he said the holy words, raising his dancing hands, he dropped the host. *"Hoc est enim corpus meum,"* he said, and then he said, "Where in hell did the goddamn son-of-a-bitch go?"

Myrtis Crawford, at any rate, was the newest victim of the duty here. He wondered, when he waved her good-by, that she had stayed above it as fully as now, remotely, she grieved over Brendan.

He went on back to the avenue which led past the front of the monastery, off toward the woods and to the perimeter road. The oaks there had often been the subject of the monastery's bad poets, hailed variously as "father," "brother," "seed." Abbot Alcuin Hegel himself had planted one of the trees and said over it, *"Carpe diem."* So the motto, though history never figured what the motto had to do with that particular oak tree. Owen laughed that the years had brought a deluge of Carpe Diem societies, the *Carpe Diem Chronicle,* the *Carpe Diem Gazette,* yearbook, the Carpe Diem scholarship fund. There was also the much spoken of Carpe Diem ring, lost in the hen house, history said.

The Carpe Diem tree stood at the very end of the avenue, and beyond was the rest of the abbey's acreage. For Owen, the fields stretched out soberly, the sun on them as though it and the land might have been also the perfect contrast between the two worlds being suddenly united.

This certainly made him think of Father Brendan, who more than anybody had spoken of loving the property. It was bred into the old priest, as with the others, that ownership had its decided merits. It suited the moment, though Owen still wasn't anything but ambivalent. Death, here, was anomalous in its treachery.

And so, Miss Hone's house seemed the best place to be now.

He walked on the several hundred yards that it took, and he found her crocheting on the porch. Filch was there bark-

106

ing. She had the habit of talking to him when she really meant to be talking to her caller.

"Is that Father Owen Cline, Filchy? Well you just tell him that I'm so happy to see him; my Annie is gone for groceries; I'm lonely and I'm just glad that he's here."

"Thank you, Miss Addie."

He told her the news immediately. She said that she thought she had heard the bell. She adjusted her hearing aid. She went on that it was a pity, but she didn't seem in the least distracted. Her eyes widened to take in her own domain. It was, for Owen, a kind of history exploding from there.

"I know all about death, and I know all about monks," she said. "Well, they all come and go."

He smiled as she whispered.

"God knows Brendan'll make it. I mean, we've got to believe in heaven, haven't we?"

She smiled almost coyly.

"He was the most vulnerable. I mean, he carried his heart on his shirt sleeves — Yes, yes, and we know he had a little trouble with his pants. What'll Myrtis do?"

"Don't know . . ."

"Well, when a woman is fool enough to love a priest . . ."

She offered him coffee this time. She brought out a white crockery urn which she said was far more the appropriate thing than the large silver one. All the while she stared with her head cocked for sound.

He folded his hands around the coffee cup and took it off its saucer.

She said, "Well, is something else wrong?"

107

"Nothing."

"Did Brendan Price mean all that much . . ."

"Hm, well, it's the time, the timing and things, and . . ."

Miss Hone was suddenly pensive in that special way which meant she was reading way beyond the situation itself.

She offered her omniscient look, but the candor as well. "Which one of the two usual problems have you got? Is it sex or is it boredom?"

Owen laughed as he usually did at her perception. She preferred not to treat him as a case; not the case who fulfilled her "come and go" definition. They had talked enough about that in the past. Here he knew she was only sensing, however; he wanted to be able to be more specific himself.

Finally he told her that it was loneliness.

To which Miss Adelaide, lovely in her sympathy, added a more than affable intensity.

"You and Anne," she whispered; her eyes took an all-knowing cast while he laughed, embarrassed.

"What if maybe something happened . . . my leuco-plakia, for instance. Anne would have somebody; you'd have somebody too." She said that she had been seeing the looks he gave Anne for a long time. She said, "And furthermore, it's not as if it was some terrible sin . . ."

She sighed and winked. "There's something else, too." She sensed the cynicism that had finally come over him. And she went to the desk in her parlor, where she took out a small, heavy, tin box with four locks on it. She opened the locks happily and pulled out a large stack of letters and some ornaments. Finally a large amethyst ring set in gold. The crest was the Carpe Diem one. The ring was Abbot Alcuin Hegel's.

"The story is that he lost this in the hen house," she said. She rubbed the ring, held it to the light as she stumbled briefly to get her footing. "I won't tell you the real story, but . . . well, when a woman loves a priest. You do understand, Abbot Hegel and I . . . *Alcuin* and I . . . my dear dear Alcuin."

Her eyes sparkled like a maiden's, but then she looked down and said, "All these years." She said, "Now I'm dying, too; the door swings open; it's only memory that endures, you know. I think that's what religion is; I mean it's the memory of your mistakes. In a way it's a comfort, too. I really have lived here all these years."

She hesitated before she said the rest:

"Annie doesn't know these things, and don't you go telling. The monks don't know. This memory is my salvation. God knows, Alcuin Hegel was better than most men, better than most Christians."

She nudged Owen. "Do you see . . . it's my index cards, it's my dog in church, it's all of that. I'm celebrating my mistakes, like the best Christians, like the monks of Boldface Abbey, ha, ha, ha."

Yet she wasn't cynical when she got down to brass tacks.

"Now you take care of Annie," the titmouse said. "And now I've got some prayers to say, and a few other items . . ."

While both the revelation and the charge stunned him, he was still fully aware that Miss Hone had gone so hastily to the back of the house that she had seemed half her age at least. All of it registered, however, in small pockets that he could easily turn inside out if he wished. Owen felt a dullness about this power as he heard the bell continuing to toll, short-circuiting, perhaps, the most significant moment he had

109

ever had. How noisy the bell sounded to him, though his concentration hadn't wavered.

And it hadn't mattered so much then, that he put in the rest of this day as most of his confreres did.

What they most wondered was how best to deal with the ceremony and the waiver of customary bans on Sunday funerals. This Abbot Giles granted in accordance with another rule that a dead monk must be buried within three days. He had wanted Vinnie Dano to be there, and he had wanted it over with.

The abbot also dutifully forewent his obligations to his friend for the space of the next anticipated evening. For this he expected time to think.

Owen and the others kept the vigil and saw to the arrangements that had to be made, the calling of relatives, and the publication of the notices to be sent to the other monasteries of the Congregation.

They did bury Brendan early that Sunday morning, in between the public Masses in the chapel. It was the abbot who preached:

Here was a man who did what monks have to do with the kind of devotion that all monks ought to have. He suffered, accepting his own weakness. Finally, he also died weakly. This is what Father Brendan believed in: immortality, simple immortality. He believed in God. That is what monks are for.

And it was at this moment that from the congregation, deep in it and buried as if she had wanted to hide, Myrtis Crawford stood angrily. She was worn and tired, though she walked with the pride of an old school teacher. She wasn't really uncontrolled though with a frenzy she walked the aisles and told them that none of it was true. She held her black purse upside down and tore at it, crying in the silence with a great remoteness, cutting herself off from the others.

And the point was that no one could go to her, that no one knew the words. Abbot Giles stammered from the pulpit, said her name, forced in this horror to see that she was hurting.

Almost everybody else gaped until she had told them as well that it was all she wanted to say. She only pleaded silently that she didn't understand, though, "Indeed," she cried, "it's not him that's got anything to worry about!"

She sat as if it had never happened; at the moment when, at last, they had brought the pall to the front to incense it, she had settled for prayer: Our Father . . . But deliver us from evil . . .

Owen Cline found Miss Hone almost smiling with understanding. He sat next to Anne and her, somehow perfectly tied to them. Miss Adelaide nodded, holding up her hand so that he could see she was wearing the Carpe Diem ring. She was then very sober as her niece wept.

Vinnie was there too. He was next to Miss Adelaide farther in the pew. He was also timid, watching the abbot, curiously aware of a new strain of commitment in him.

The monks sang the "Dies Irae" in Latin because Father Affirmo insisted that Brendan would have preferred it. This priest, rarely able to show emotion in ceremonies, carried out his duties as master of ceremonies as if he were blaming everybody for the death. He angrily ordered the altar boys, wildly taking off and replacing the abbot's mitre.

In the cemetery they sang the "Ultima," the customary farewell in the name of the Virgin. They gave the Asperges. The wooden coffin was lowered deferentially.

Finally it was a matter of the other farewells that had to take place.

The abbot stood alongside Vinnie, who shook his hand and said that he would be back next weekend. Father Affirmo and Father Phineas took care of Father Brendan's few relatives. And they took care of Myrtis Crawford who arrived late at the burial and stood outside the canopy.

They resisted telling her that she was out of place to have broken her way into the monastery, to have made a fool of herself in church.

It was Abbot Giles, thinking of Vinnie and his lights, who finally went to her and told her that he was risking everything to say it, but, "There'll always be a place for you here."

Her gaze, which now surveyed the scene passively, sank as her hands did. She took the aspergil and squeezed it and threw a little water over the top of the descending casket. She thanked the abbot, looking at the monks standing around one by one. She smiled at them, knowing that they were finally disposed to forgive her. Under her breath she praised Brendan, she called to him in baby talk. The monks shook her hand while she thought of him over her like a tank, breathing his acid breath. She thanked God, as *he* would have on such occasions.

FOURTEEN   FROM THERE the steam was gathering only slowly for the next weekend, which promised special significance for the abbot and monks of Boldface Abbey. It was the founding abbot's birthday weekend. Some said, "Too bad that Brendan didn't live . . ."

"Yes, and too bad he didn't live especially to see the new monastery some day."

But they of course continued to plan Saturday and Sunday as festival days the way they had always done. They dragged out the old photographs and all the museum pieces. They had founding Abbot Alcuin Hegel's chalice, for example, and his hyssop. And they put out these articles in a hallway of the college, in a display case that they borrowed from the Roses Stores.

There would be a picnic and lawn party. Miss Adelaide Hone traditionally made a gelatin mold of a design that celebrated something from history. She had already sent out word this year that the design would be significant.

They buzzed about it curiously, having the word out

113

now that she was dying. She reminded them every day at daily noon Mass, filling them in on the details in the vestibule, "Leucoplakia at eighty-six. I've done two heart attacks, but now this. Look, see, tsk, tsk, I'll show you."

Father Affirmo fell perfectly into her trap, said, "The end of an era, the last of the old guard; the titmouse is crawling to her hole to die . . ."

Phineas commiserated genuinely: "For the funeral I'll play the 'Anvil Chorus.' "

The flavor of things, thereby, had bothered Father Owen Cline most, since he now couldn't help acknowledging the protection in talk like that. For one thing it kept them off Brendan's death. Owen's energy was spent in trying to feel sorry for Miss Hone too.

And then he had a moment of triumph, putting Brendan aside altogether, preferring to notice, as they all did, that Myrtis Crawford had returned to work in the college library, where she wore her distant smile and new clothes. In Miss Hone's behalf he kept the little card, which she sent out announcing the significance of her mold, propped on the bureau. There the card was a reminder of his most precious triumph as well.

He thought of Anne and of Miss Hone's intimations. But he felt drawn to distinctions which, like insomnia itself, brought him too readily to detest his fantasies. Now the real issue was clear-cut while he, for instance, remembered that there was once a girl named Helen Kirkus who lived next door to his family when he was in grade school; and she had a friend named Johnny Dudisell who lived in the house next to that. When they were children, Helen Kirkus invited him and the other neighborhood children out to the brush pile

114

where she and Johnny Dudisell charged ten cents to see them get down into the creek bed on top of each other. Owen had this set in his senses. He regretted losing his dime, though now the whole thing haunted him as if it had been the single epiphany that had sent him, at nineteen, to the monastery. The new thing was that, in these moments, the priesthood seemed more an escape than ever. He touched himself thinking of Father Olaf Dotis's words: "There are those who have made themselves eunuchs . . ." and so forth.

The image of his own possible impotency drummed away and then he wished dreadfully that he were not having such triumphs.

Of course, that was the worst of it, even in the pleasant, useless fantasy — he meant the silliness, too; he shouldn't possibly feel anything from Miss Hone's connivances.

When he found himself arriving ahead of time at the opening ceremonies for Founder's Day, he disliked both the premise and the expectation in the new-found hope.

But he maintained the hope, and the ceremonies began with Abbot Giles arriving in his red buskins. This didn't please the young. It did please Affirmo who also insisted that Giles wear the capa with the bearskin collar. He had brought out the best copies of the *CEREMONIALES,* having pasted the new English translations onto the pages of the old Latin text.

So, the lengthy Mass, all the remembrances, the special music that Father Phineas had written for two trumpets. There was supposed to be no entrance, but Phineas put one in anyhow, upsetting Affirmo in his attempt, as master of ceremonies, to keep the thing moving along.

For Owen this part was interminable. All the while, his

115

eyes were fixed on Miss Hone's place and on Anne next to her, there like a plangent trumpet, he thought. Then, at last, that afternoon he met her over the pickle dish at the reunion table. He was pleased that she wore her sunglasses, her Italian sun hat, her seersucker blouse.

She had that European look about her, all-knowing, he told her, though she dropped her head sadly, half-smiling, uncertain of his behavior.

She said, "I'm a little angry and very much disturbed that everybody takes things in such stride. Everybody knows that Father Brendan died; and now Aunt Adelaide is . . ."

He saw this as an opportunity to please her.

"Even Miss Addie herself says that people come and go . . ."

"It's almost as if they were waiting . . ."

"They are . . ."

They sat under a nearby magnolia because Anne didn't want to be far from her aunt. Her light yellow blouse was caught by the elastic of a matching skirt. He saw that the pleats of her skirt helped to hide a lace slip that was too long. He felt free to notice, catching Miss Hone's encouraging nods in their direction.

Finally Anne was smiling, but not a full smile. She watched her aunt, who held court like Scarlett O'Hara. And then Miss Hone brought out her surprise mold.

This time it was a bright red one in the shape of a ring, the Carpe Diem ring. She looked at Owen coyly, and he winked back, daring to touch Anne's shoulder. Miss Hone lifted the mold as though in consecration, walking unsteadily to the abbot who sipped punch at the reunion table, expecting Vinnie Dano at any moment.

116

There she handed over the mold ceremoniously, winking over and over again; making Giles uncomfortable and suspicious. He smiled, not knowing really what to do, took the mold, smiling further at her. Miss Hone abruptly told him that she had something to say. She said, first, that she wasn't afraid of leucoplakia. Not afraid of death, and she was sorry to be abrupt about it, though already she had planned to say it.

"Surely you've all heard that it's the big C." Her little hands twitched as she stared upward toward the nearby parapet at the end of the Boldface Institute Administration Building.

"The Carpe Diem ring ought to be the symbol of something. Boldface Abbey is still standing, you see."

She said that, yes, she knew her monks; that there had to be a way to heaven. "Here's a way, I suppose."

She looked from monk to monk. "God knows, you've made enough mistakes. What I mean is that here's something that keeps going while everything else dies. It's better than being only human, and we have to make sure of it . . ."

She had quickly motioned the abbot to stand next to her, and he went reluctantly, fearful that it would be another humiliation in her set of games. But she almost embraced him, looking a little sad, assuring him as if in forgiveness. He sighed heavily.

"And I want to tell you," she said, "and don't let this surprise you because the abbot, here, and I've been discussing it, and . . . well, I'm planning to go to the bank tomorrow, and I'm going to instruct the banker to give the abbot the money for his new monastery. He'll name it, of course, after

Abbot Hegel. He'll soon break ground for it . . . and that's that."

She had rested as though taking a bow, wrestling to the last with the suitability of it. And they were all lively as they came up to the nonplussed abbot, who let himself smile and embrace her, watched her stalwartly, like the church, go off again to her corner to hold court.

He waited more intensely for Vinnie now, and seeing him then come into the front parking lot, went quickly with the news. If the week's constraints had worn more on Miss Hone and the others — her decision and the other events — they had worn less on Giles. He told Vinnie almost immediately, "Nothing has changed." All along Giles remembered the scene that had just ended, thinking Miss Hone suddenly prophetical, himself the learner in all the recent situations. Brendan Price was on his mind, too, and the advance of life itself: the door swinging open and the door swinging closed. It was right and wrong that there was no formula for it.

Then he saw that, at the festivity, Vinnie was remote and displeased. The dark and amusing smile was gone and Vinnie fidgeted with his shirt collar.

He didn't see Giles, momentarily without burdens, as Giles saw himself. Nor had he been happy to see that Giles put on a face that baffled even Affirmo who had come to the feast and stood as usual at the fringe of things saying, "One more damn silly bit of nonsense to make people think he's doing his job."

The only ones to note Affirmo were Owen Cline and Anne Hone. She refused to smile when he told her that Affirmo certainly hadn't meant that literally, and then that Abbot Giles must certainly be happy; at last to be keeping up with the changing times.

FIFTEEN   WHICH MEANT that the time wore on in the resplendence of this Georgia afternoon and wore on midst the mingling of old parishioners who celebrated each year by renewing their hearsay stories about Abbot Hegel. As it was Miss Hone alone among them who really knew whatever was to be known, those who had something to say preferred not to say it in her presence. The Carpe Diem ring was the subject. Now they said, "Wonder how Miss Adelaide knows what she knows?" But they always said that.

She was under her magnolia keeping her court. The young boys who were sons of the older men and women fetched her food; the older men admired her dog. She smiled, content at last, and kept an eye on Anne who now let herself relax a little too. Though it was difficult being followed around by Owen Cline.

He was bold enough to say, "What are you going to do, I mean . . . when Miss Hone has . . . what *are* you going to do?"

She said, "Remarks like that make me angry, Father Owen."

They sat under another magnolia. The gathering dwindled as they sat without talking further until Anne had told him about her particular sadness, about the things that Miss Hone meant to her.

"For example, she's the dearest example of somebody who's done the battle well. All these years living here and keeping Boldface the most important part of her life."

"An unfortunate part," he said.

"No, Father, no; no more than *your* interest here."

"I've no interest here."

She looked at him inertly. The vision she had was of his strange behavior in the confessional all these years.

"I really don't want to hear about it . . ."

"Well, it's not as if I'd told you anything . . . I . . ."

"I know what you're thinking."

"Listen," said Owen, "don't you think we could at least talk about it?"

"There's nothing to talk about."

She stretched her legs forward and stared at her feet, dangling them at last off the bench. He told her that, funny, this bench was the place where Boldface Abbey students usually made love. Father Olaf Dotis kept watch on the goings-on here; he often had the bench removed.

"You don't know anything about love," she said.

"And I suppose you do?"

"As a matter of fact, yes."

Her mind was on the rest of what Anne Hone most carefully guarded about herself and her detachment. Yes, the sun was high above her and she trusted the deep identification she made with the air and with the little jets of heat that passed like whispers over her naked arms. She was stirred splendidly by the containment which there held her distant from what she did understand in Owen's face and in his movements. She might even have been attracted to him but for what she loved about being expertly remote. First, she liked merely sitting there, then being committed to nothing but that. She sensed Owen's obsessions, then, a tiring momentum as though too much might have hinged on her responses.

"Have you ever traveled?" she said.

"No," he said.

"You should. Life elsewhere is more . . . primitive. Take Europe, where the people have more . . . ease of soul, perhaps more vices . . ."

"Should people have more vices?"

"I'd think that you'd understand that. There're things people have to do because they can't bear the pain otherwise. There are two kinds of people, Father: those who live with ignorance, and those whose passions won't move except in one direction."

She liked teasing him. She pitied him only slightly, and when he didn't answer, she told him what she thought might make more sense.

"I used to live in Spain where the sky is different from the Georgia sky. You can see an orange in the clouds always. The hillsides glow like El Greco paintings. There are a lot of churches. There are lots of people but you never really see them because they don't treat every minute of the day as if it were the last. I learned this from them. You're provincial, Father Owen. You're serious and angry as I used to be. Then I worked at my studies without any comfort until they didn't mean anything. All along, I was feeling something

121

about the outside things I saw, the world. It was stretching itself out for me slowly. I had only a spark of an overpowering interest in the sunlight then, in roads, in trees and animals. Finally, I felt myself merely beside these things. Now I feel a part of them. It's settled me. It's what Aunt Addie has, what you monks ought to have, ha, ha . . ."

And he said that he didn't understand. He told her outright that Miss Adelaide herself had made him promise to take care of her. He said that she said "It's for you and Anne." Then he laughed sheepishly and she said he was silly again.

But that wasn't the end of any of what either of them felt, though Anne repeated that she knew what love was. It could be practiced or abused in the name of many things. She said that she knew, but she wasn't going to talk about it.

He said, "But don't you understand that I'm telling you something; don't you see my unhappiness; haven't you been able to see . . ."

"I'm not really interested," she said. "What I have to tell you is this: you have to exhaust all of what you think pleasure is. It forces you elsewhere. I'm at that point. I've come to that point and I know."

"How do you know?"

It seemed to him that her face gleamed with extraordinary knowledge. It was the privilege of women, he thought, guarding all the former premises about her, their reasons for never having got beyond this point; in fact, he was able to regard getting this far as something monumental. For the moment he didn't think of his own weaknesses, the fear of her which had kept him from really saying what he thought.

Then he said, "Suppose I loved you . . . Suppose, I mean, that I *thought* I loved you?"

122

"Ha, ha."

Then she said, "Well, I barely know you, for one thing."
She looked away toward the perimeter road watching members of the gathering going away, older ones like her aunt.
She saw an old man and an old woman, their clothes bright against the late sun. She couldn't recall having seen them at the lawn party.

She said, "Well, if you must know, Father Owen, I'm pleased to be happy. Except for the sorrow I'll have when Aunt Addie dies, there's nothing that I fear or dread. My answer to that is with what I've told you. I've had my loves, you know."

Of all the pretense, he thought. He wasn't even sure of what he expected of her then; for once, he wanted to remember her confessions.

Then he wasn't able even to think Miss Hone above these matters. How she railed against the abbot, against the way things were.

And then they were at her court for good. She had motioned them, and Anne encouraged him there where they spent the rest of the afternoon, until dusk, fielding questions for her. Each had by this time thought that mutual silence called attention to something further, too, but Miss Hone hadn't allowed it.

Owen said good-by to her thinking that this couldn't be all. And Miss Hone also said, "You must come by Sunday for a chat again."

Anne Hone only smiled with a lingering idea of his having been too much a child. She knew he felt small. And he was angry.

SIXTEEN   ABBOT GILES was still trying to adjust to Miss Hone's announcement. At the lawn party he had more or less continued to roam with the crowd, letting the news seep through. It hadn't even dawned on him completely when it was time to thank Miss Hone and say good-by to her. Thus it was in a perfunctory manner that he could smile and assure her that it excited him and certainly he would give her all the proper credit. Even with Vinnie in his room afterward, he marked time against the possible rescinding of it, against its being a dream.

But then it was a matter of his coming to the full realization. His eyes wide, settled in, a drink poured, and Vinnie looking at him stolidly, he almost cried the thing out: "I've done it, I've done it, I've done it."

Vinnie said, "Calm yourself."

"But, Vin, now they will remember me . . . now they will care about me, and . . . A toast, Vin, to the restoration of Boldface Abbey . . . to Alcuin Hegel."

Giles wasn't just to leave it at that either; the exuber-

124

ance, the forgiveness got to him ecstatically, and he sent for Affirmo and Owen.

"Those two as good as any — I'd like a toast to an old monk and a young monk; they represent them all, you see. Then, Vinnie, we must talk, mustn't we."

And laughing still, he toasted a miffed Affirmo, who became noticeably annoyed that this was the reason he had been invited in.

He said, "I wouldn't expect too much too soon."

But Owen had watched the abbot, trying for a little commiseration. "We could have the ground-breaking any moment. We could even have it tomorrow, or . . ."

"Where are we going to put it, then?" Affirmo asked with a smirk. "We haven't even talked about where the damn thing is going to go. What about that!"

He smoked a cigarette with his drink, only tasting it and grunting. What was all this nonsense about a mess that couldn't be settled in any move less than Giles's resignation? He kept on, "It almost seems a mockery, and I, for one . . ."

"Come on, Affirmo," the abbot said, "come on and enjoy yourself for once in your life."

"You can't build a monastery without a place to put it," the archivist said.

Even Owen said, "Father, that really is the least of the problems."

But Affirmo was worse than annoyed now. His face was showing the old Affirmo Biggsbee: eyes moving rapidly, a bigger smirk, the final inability to be comfortable. He looked at Owen and Giles and Vinnie as if they had been there only to serve his contempt. They were culprits to him.

"I didn't come for this," he said, lighting another ciga-

125

rette. It was final; he was unaware of his deeper urges because he never saw the world but in small representations of better things. Even the better things, it seemed, were tainted by personalities and factions. He was thinking: I have outlived my usefulness, remembering the days when the old liturgy had been in and Abbot Wilfrid had put him totally in charge. Everybody ought to remember him moving like a fox in and out of the ceremonies and making jokes in the meantime. He really had wanted to be an abbot. Two of his novitiate confreres had become abbots elsewhere, and he lamented that he couldn't write them letters, as they did him, with an abbot's seal at the top. He loathed Giles's memos for this reason. The white embossed stationery might have been his.

Affirmo thought that cleverness was his salvation. The jokes were cleverer now that he was older. And all the misanthropic elements were collecting here in this intensity. Present company seemed the most singular picture of his frustration.

Yet he knew that Abbot Giles was too pleased with Miss Hone's bequest and with his own accomplishment.

"There's the door, Father Affirmo," he said. "This is a celebration, and if you don't like it . . ."

Affirmo chose the moment carefully. "You ambitious bastard." He felt released to say it. "You and your silly impertinences, mismanagements. *You* are the ill of this place. You and your . . ." (he looked at Vincent Dano smugly) ". . . *friend.*"

The old man's hands were shaking, his eyes set wildly on the abbot's. At that he had left still much unsaid.

He thought of the way he wanted to say it, letting go

126

where he might not have questioned the abbot's authority. It was something about the time, the place, the abbot's manner.

But Giles was angry. He said, "I am your legitimate superior; you will not speak to me in this fashion!"

He couldn't think otherwise. He let the silence crest over his words, looking helplessly toward Vinnie, who laughed out loud. Who said, "Well, that's that. That solves every problem in the world."

And Affirmo went out shaking as Owen grimaced. Owen had yet another sense of the absurdity of the situation. Then he had to leave in embarrassment also, watching the abbot tremble and face Vinnie with full sadness, furious. Owen noted with growing hostility that Giles now represented something frail to him, though unquestionably as distasteful as the source of his embarrassment: he imagined Giles's game like his own.

With Affirmo and Owen gone, Giles looked at his friend with added regret. He said, "Should I go after them?"

Vinnie said, "Hell no, let them go. Let them all go. *You* ought to go."

He paced with his drink and said that he hadn't come again for any such foolishness as this. The whole business with the Hone money was silly. "I mean, you people live together but you really don't know each other. I don't know what it is that keeps you together; I can't imagine what good a new building would do when such as this goes on."

What quickly erased Giles's concern about the matter was his enjoyment of Vinnie's sudden intensity. It was the old Vinnie, in a sense, who often used to get upset like this; stood in that very spot and beat his hand in his fist and said that it was all futile; what the hell point at all was there in the so-

127

called human dilemma when, in fact, the trap disappears when you talk about it. How Giles loved the cautious mind behind statements like that. Now Vinnie also had a curious resignation, he thought. The problem, thus, might have been more superficial than he supposed and he didn't mind having his friend see him in a moment of weakness. The truth was that now Giles and Vinnie *did* have something new to talk about and Owen and Affirmo didn't matter.

For this it was even more exciting that Giles's mind trailed off toward the lights which were a momentary guide both to his feelings and to his self-image. He looked at himself standing like a mirror in the snow. He was sweating and felt the water going along his body inside his clothes. He was fixed again in remoteness though he fought to peer at himself around the edges of the externals.

He said nothing else to Vinnie, and gathered up a clean towel and fresh underwear and went into the bathroom. He took off his habit piece by piece, letting himself be aware of the feel of his garments. He got into the shower easily. The fantasies were of a protracted sense of touch.

He remembered the deranged woman at Lauds, the singular cold disgust in Affirmo's face, Owen Cline's fickleness, poor dead Brendan whom he hadn't understood.

He dressed slowly then and returned to Vinnie, who was unconcerned. He was dreaming, himself, of being in motion. He had put in the week with the usual things. This was his agitation: those who were really sick were incurably so, and those who weren't incurably sick didn't need him. But not that alone. It was the phantom of greed that troubled him; words again like duty and dependence; finally system and structure as well. Himself. For he knew it in the patient

128

whose stroke left him speechless and jobless. A woman had showed up that week who had actually begged him to say that she was mentally unstable so that she could be committed and avoid an upcoming divorce. Even now: Giles, dedicated to these petty quarrels and trivia.

Vinnie didn't care. This time he had almost set off for someplace where even Giles wouldn't find him.

But the abbot by this time was sitting behind his desk again. He wasn't looking at the monastery plans; he was rubbing his hand softly against them. The abbot's eyes were fixed on Vinnie's eyes.

He raised his glass and drank, swallowing and then playing with a piece of ice in his mouth. He did this twice. Then Abbot Giles got up and came forward. He first touched Vinnie's arms, and Vinnie didn't do anything. The abbot knelt down, letting his hands fall to Vinnie's knees. He rubbed the knees softly.

Vinnie Dano returned these touches without control. Friction itself was the allurement. Giles's breath droned at him pitifully. For both of them it went on like that world toward which each felt himself ultimately bound. Where lights and sounds were the language and where neither needed worry about the formula for it.

SEVENTEEN   SUNDAY MORNING and Founder's Day.
Even the holly bushes standing in the forefront like the
magnolias behind them, and the azaleas just in bloom,
cowered to the rain, a quiet rain as if in the swish of a
dehumidifier. The sun came in sportive moments. The
ballet dancing mimosa flowerets were on the ground and
bathed in oil from leaking monastery automobiles. The oil
itself forming its erratic rainbows against the rill in an old
stone in the driveway where the monastery cars were kept.
And ripening Georgia peach trees untended, Judas trees
unpruned, pomegranate bushes perplexed against lacy weeds.
Morning Mass; people arriving with umbrellas in modish
styles to become a loop of children's cereal engulfed by the
huge mouth of the chapel's doors; and God in his heaven.

"Get up, John Vincent Dano," the abbot said. "Get up,
oh dear and glorious physician. I'm going to talk to you
about sonship. I have also written something in my journal.
Let me read it: Lord, had I the sense to know it, I should
first have cried out to humanity.

"How do you like it?"

Vinnie let his arm fall off the abbot's bed, its muscles loosened by deep yawning and the quick turn. His eyes somehow misshaped by a small grin, imperceptible except to Abbot Giles who traced his finger lightly there.

Vinnie laughed out loud against the abbot's shushes that there might be prowling hearers.

The abbot was in his shorts and was shaving at the stand next to the bed.

"The bathroom's yours."

He crossed the razor against the shaving mug and made a cross. "I will go, I will go to the altar of God."

"What shit *is* this?" Vinnie said. He threw back the sheets, finding himself naked. He scratched as the abbot looked on and they exchanged a glance which then spoke best of the evening before. It was a half smile, however, which drew them together again. They heard the rain, its subdued rhythm.

Father Affirmo was saying the morning public Mass for the people, blending voice with reserve, the words sharply determined to be a service to duty and to divinity. He moved like a man with a braced back, made his crosses in perfect symmetry, though hastily.

The sermon:

We can but mention the few who represent the hundreds of church fathers and teachers who have regarded the human ordeal as a trial for something far greater than the reward seems, momentarily, to promise. But you cannot imagine, my dear people, how immeasurable that reward. Do you not sometimes fear that it has gotten to be too much for you? I know this feeling. Holy Writ, you know, first says that we are to expect trial and tribulation; but then Holy Writ im-

131

mediately follows up and says that God will never tempt us beyond what we are capable of bearing. The truth is that God does not tempt us at all. Weak natures.

God knows, and we know, that we are the cause of our own evil, our own vile acts. We are the ones who do evil. This is what Holy Writ, as I have said, tells us. Sin is a fact of life, isn't it?

He did the lavabo with a little cross as if he might be trying to sneak up on it.

When he was done the monks came in for the delayed Sunday Lauds. Festive Lauds. Abbot Wilfrid was on assignment; the sub-prior was sleeping in. It was up to Affirmo to sound the starting bell, which he did reluctantly, seeing that the abbot was absent.

For the festivity they had planned the Office in Latin, for old time's sake, and returning to it now, most chanted with only a remembrance of tones and pointings. Nostalgia pervaded the smiles that recognized this, and since the rubrics were not written in the customary red, they chanted them too: *In manum dextrum sacerdos tenet librum.*

Father Phineas drowsily began to look for the place in the Book, as it was his time to read. He was tired and had forgotten that it was his turn. Not uncharacteristically, three of the monks tried whispering the place to him. Affirmo himself said the page number out loud.

Phineas said, "Keep your shirt on," and they grimaced and looked to see that no one heard. Still it went out on the microphone and Phineas said, "For Godssakes, will you give me the time to find the damn thing." The people averted their faces.

Owen Cline was there. He hadn't slept, supposing that it was the crawling indifference. Perhaps Anne Hone. His mind shifted to her from time to time, and he sat in his place, stared upon by the faces of the stained-glass saints. Saint Bernard, for example, with a joyous face, arms up in a ballet dancer's halo, fingers heavenward; Saint Walburgha with folded arms, her piercing eyes like a disgruntled school teacher's; and then dear Saint Cunigunda with the far-reaching look; all of them engulfing the bodies of partially clothed sinners who carried aloft representative tokens of their sins: one with money, one with an ear, another with an eye, and the last bearing up a blazing heart. Where was the place for the inveterately bored?

In the back, the partly deaf Father Egbert was hearing confessions.

"My son, your sins are making me sick."

A darkly clad woman emerged with visible embarrassment, turning her heels quickly into the last pew, kneeling reverently.

Elsewhere the rain was soaking up the oncoming heat, and the deep green of midsummer came up like a child on the silent morning's back. It was carried fast toward the heavens and toward the loftiest point of the chapel spire where the gold cross, dulled without sun, had taken the land as its own, pulling it and straining it by the force of its height.

The festival emerged.

This was the day for a procession where everyone would gather en masse at the chapel door, and they would follow the abbot, with the Blessed Sacrament in reserve, around the Abbey's circumference. They would stop at stations on the way, through the woods, and say special prayers in the founding abbot's honor.

133

The rain finally stopped. The trumpeters were there, and the abbot had come out wearing red. He carried the capa, which had been granted in perpetuum to the successors of Abbot Hegel, in a bundle around him, the ancient bear skin mantle losing its fur, bits of it sticking in the abbot's mouth. He smiled, his face especially radiant. This bursting energy was communicated. Monks were coming awake; the Office was in its last stage.

They wakened further to hear Abbot Giles giving orders to get the oldest vessels ready; the umbrellina up there and dusted, for Godssakes, the six silver lamps drawn from the attic storage. They brought forth gold-plated candlesticks and put them on the floor where, even there, they dwarfed the makeshift wooden altar facing the people.

He had vested himself in the best lace rochet, last of all taping up the two-large headband of Abbot Hegel's mitre. He brought with him the old man's chalice, heavy with rubies.

"Let's get this show on the road."

Affirmo, dressing for the master of ceremonies role, was showing mixed feelings. He still couldn't see Giles Logan really looking the part of a prelate.

"Another damn thing!"

Giles tweaked his nose.

"Now move it," he said. He positioned the altar boys himself, told them how far behind to walk with the capa. "You in back stay up with us now."

In the main, he generated valor in them all. The sun out, they started from the rear of the church around to the front. They took the road to the cemetery and then the pathways where the mud caught them unawares. It made no difference to Abbot Giles.

The woods to him were tropical; rain water dripped off the pines and the oaks like jewels, he fancied, and the stones of his mitre, he hoped, joined them in an elegance they hadn't seen for half a century. The paths hadn't been weeded, nor had the many stations along them where the procession was going been set upright. These stations, each hand-carved and representing a saint who had been good to the Order, were made by the same lay brothers who had built the monastery and college buildings. In those days there had been over sixty of these brothers. They had cleared the land and made the pathways. Their stations lay on the ground with rot, and the abbot, passing by, swore that the new Bold-face Abbey would not have this waste.

It ended when they trudged back soaked with rain water and covered with mud. The abbot, still exuberant, carried his crosier high, in front, where he liked to be. The others, including Adelaide Hone and her niece, complained of the mud. But Miss Adelaide was curiously faithful, smiling at him, supposing that he now knew what she did about religion.

Even Affirmo wrung out his surplice with a minimum of complaint.

"The next will be to break ground for the new monastery," Giles said loudly. He noted first that Vinnie's automobile was gone from the parking lot.

He was sad now, watching his monks disperse, watching Miss Hone sidle off like a specter, Owen Cline go quickly to his room. Affirmo lighted his cigarette.

The festival was over.

135

EIGHTEEN   IN THE DARK of his room the abbot still reveled in his disposition of matters, aware and not aware that little had actually changed with any of them. The real thing was his thought of Vinnie; and then his option of building, now that the money was guaranteed. He would have to have the ground-breaking soon, just a token, at least, and he called up Miss Adelaide and said, "Now don't joke with me and don't pretend one way or the other. I must know."

She confirmed that it was in excess of a million that she had to offer, and said she thought maybe he was finally coming of age. "You'll never be an Abbot Hegel, but I noticed today that you had a little *sprezzatura;* that's Italian for guts." The voice was lively; she significantly pleased. She even said that she was willing to forget bygone disagreements and refreshed the abbot on their differences.

"It was your general stupidity. You treat religion as if it really had to mean something. Forget the meaning and get down to the act. You did fairly well, as Christians go. My niece, devout truly," she whispered, "believed it."

It puzzled him, of course, but he said that it wasn't merely that he was doing it for Boldface, but for all the time that they'd suffered together.

"This new building is going to be in honor of Abbot Hegel or not at all!" she said.

He didn't resent the implication. He said, "Yes, yes," to that, feeling grateful and trying genuinely to tell her about it.

"Stand by for the ground-breaking," he said. "We'll let you know."

He anticipated the visit to the bank; he anticipated a vast number of cheerful meetings with the architects and with his own confreres at which, he swore, he would win their affection.

Then he thought exclusively of Vinnie.

So they hadn't parted with any promises. Vinnie had only said, "Well." Nor had they really talked, because the subject hadn't been one that either could find a vocabulary to deal with. The terms were forbidding, as Giles imagined they must have to be, for it was a discovery that horrified him. Yet his insides had possessed a contentment unlike anything he had ever known. It gave him the happiness of the procession, the courage to deal with Miss Hone, he thought. His mind sailed along on less remote courses and still the waving strain of something distant had made it seem unreal. This wasn't unpleasant; it was only distracting.

He had embraced Vinnie before he had left his room, the cry of his former remoteness dying, but replaced by a still more electric dependency. He didn't know how he had ever known that word. He was content in levels of closeness to the moment when he felt loved, though he could feel it fading. This he didn't dwell on, but he was desperately looking forward to next weekend. He didn't want, really, to consider

137

the meaning of Vinnie's having left without saying anything further.

But he must keep up the new leadership. He was constrained just then to call in Fathers Affirmo and Owen and apologize for that awful outburst of temper, "Well, Fathers, that silliness in my being tired, things getting to me, you know . . ."

He did it against the backdrop of the predilections he thought each had. He was aware of Owen's sluggishness for, perhaps, the first time. He felt Affirmo's presence like a weight, and the older man hadn't said anything. He sat on the sofa with his legs crossed and his head up, powerful.

A summer free from teaching obligations put them into that frame of mind that Giles wanted to recognize as indifference. The regular problem was that the monks really had little to do at this time of the year, and he was seeing the boredom, he thought. He himself had always used the summer profitably, going to take a few courses. Affirmo held that in contempt. Owen, with only a master's in education, hadn't needed anything else.

Point was that these facts had only crossed his desk in a kind of perfunctory way, and Giles didn't really regard them as touchy subjects. Yet he knew that Affirmo, mysteriously, would.

"Isn't there *something* we can talk together about?" he said, trying to laugh.

Owen said, "I, for one, am pleased that Miss Hone has made her decision."

The abbot looked at Affirmo, who got up on the spot and left indignantly.

Owen and Giles didn't speak. It was partly that each

recognized that he hadn't talked privately to the other for years. In Owen's mind was Giles's strange inconsistency. And Giles, displeased with Affirmo, infuriated with him, strained to be adequately indulgent.

"Well, then," he said, "what a character!"

Owen wanted to say it then, and he did: "Old bored fool!" And he found himself thinking that monks found each others' faults like animals guarding territorial imperatives. Affirmo knew that silence was a weapon; he had used it like a war lord. It seemed clear that they were so close to each other, and yet no one of them seemed to know anything really about the other. Giles, apparently, couldn't tell what was happening. In the old days the regimen minimized any quarrels that might have kept them at each other's throats. Recreations were planned; each man had to account for every moment of his day, and, in the service called Culpa, confess hatreds and misgivings. Somehow, it was a healthier atmosphere than in these days when everybody was left to his own devices. Now Owen knew that Abbot Giles was reacting especially to the language of his remark.

"God only knows what's to be done . . . I've wracked *my* pitiful brain . . ."

He caught himself thinking it was Vinnie when Owen replied and told him that he thought the whole proposition was getting rotten, that monasticism was something near death. In fact, that he, of all people, was frightened for his own soul!

The abbot's face had lightened. He was at ease. He wasn't aware of the deeper issues. This wasn't, to be sure, the picture of Father Owen Cline that *he* had. Owen was always a young zealot, he thought. Owen didn't worry about the

139

follies of life, the *scrutiniums* said. Giles might even have imagined him shallow. Maybe even another Affirmo, burning the candle at both ends for all his youth, and then . . .

The truth was that now Owen was finally letting it well up into anger; though merely limp, he didn't see himself actually talking to the abbot about his problems. For unconscionable reasons, Anne Hone was in his thoughts as though she did, after all, offer some kind of cure for all of what namelessly attacked him. He was touching her, perhaps, and strangely remembering her almost convincing awareness of a believable universe; her place next to the numbers of other objects, the weight of it. And this was no longer pretentious, it seemed, when weighed against the likes of Affirmo or Giles, especially himself.

Abbot Giles said, "Then, what is *your* gripe?"

Owen told him that he didn't know what his gripe was. He was determined not to appear silly and he tried casually to say the word. It came out: "I'm just not happy here."

"Oh, ha, ha, ha, ha . . ."

"I'm bored, a child. I've no desire to do anything. I'm also frightened."

"A monastery isn't supposed to be *that* kind of happy, Father."

And Owen stood as the abbot's laughter became explosive.

"Father Owen, Father Owen, please now . . . I don't mean to be flippant . . . it's just that everybody's saying it . . . it's worked its way down the ladder, it's . . ."

Owen felt then a brutal surge of contempt for himself and the situation. He could see himself only getting cynical about it in the extreme and so he yelled out loud about what was really bothering him, about the horror of his sin.

140

"I'm worn out with it. I've no control over it, and it's the only pleasure there is . . ."

That crumbled the abbot's power. He himself suddenly had to think of his own sin, of Vinnie, and pleasure. He just hadn't taken the time to consider. And it was almost as if the messengers that Brendan Price used to talk about had selected Owen to remind him. He should have been ready at once to play the role of the moralist, to have gotten out all the books with the proper advice and formulas: this, *this,* of all sins, the worst habit for a monk to fall into, this the exclusive gesture of contempt for the most precious of the monastic vows!

What remained was only Giles's subtle urge to encourage Owen and forget that they lived under strictures which they imposed upon themselves. But what of the implications of these statutes were they not imposed? Giles saw himself at the very top of the hangman's list.

He didn't want Owen there anymore. He would have cried out. To Vinnie first. But now to God, now to the everlasting principle of all things which had kept from him the knowledge of his own weakness.

He might have damned God, and the single relief was finally to have written it in his journal.

For this, Abbot Giles hurried to send Owen away without explanation. He didn't think of what he said, though the terror showed on his face. And Owen, thinking that his own words had been quite as loathsome to the abbot as they had been to himself, went away. He saw it as his own censure, which could be expected, but he also saw Abbot Giles coming apart with that strange duplicity that others always said he had.

141

NINETEEN AND FOR THAT, Owen deprecated even his
footsteps in the hallway. The ancient pine floors didn't
receive him graciously as they did in the daytime, as the noise
doubled in the floor's dominoed construction that came off
louder in the dark. And also the statue of Abbot Hegel just
outside the abbot's door: its whispers, the orange insect-
repellent bulb shining on his face.

He rushed to get outside and breathe. The air had
cleared; he caught his breath to the rhythms of draining rain
spouts, counted moments with the spasms of his bloated colon.

And this time Miss Adelaide's house drew him as if it
were far more than just proper. The lights were still on and
music came from the parlor window. Anne answered the
door, shushing him politely.

"She and the dog have gone to bed. We waited tea for
you, and Aunt Addie was disappointed, but she's gone to bed
now."

He had forgotten, he said, and he said oh that it was a
funny routine. "Yes . . . and . . ."

142

She was listening to her aunt's old Gershwin records.

"I was reading . . . About yesterday, I do so hope you understand."

She looked at him with a little distress, feeling sorry, he supposed. She felt closer, she said, now that things were out in the open. Anne hadn't meant to be blunt with him at all and she told him that she watched him during the rest of the lawn party playing a part that she seldom got to play.

"I do like to be authoritative," she said. "I do like to be superior, but I meant what I said . . . Won't you come in, Father Owen?"

He stood in the tiny room, amid the fern plants everywhere, the heavily pictured walls, amid so many prizes of which, at one time or another, Miss Hone had explained the origin in detail. He always found the house quaint, a delicate smell that wasn't quite perfume lingering like the taste of rosewater.

At this point he might have thought better of himself too.

"But I don't want you to misunderstand."

"I really came to apologize," he said.

"And that's infantile. Why can't you just be yourself? It's never very easy to be above your own fears."

He sat on the sofa and she got him a glass of wine without asking him first. She sat next to him, leaning on her elbow against the back of the sofa. She deliberately kept her eyes downcast. She was uncomfortable though he looked at her guilelessly. He knew this, and had nothing to fight about, and he wasn't thinking anything more.

"I'm just here, present, *adsum,* whatever. It's been a bad day."

143

He told her everything about Giles and about what he had said to him. All of it. He told her that he felt cooped up and would never get to that point she talked about. The worst of it issued as though she might have had special powers to absolve him. But only Miss Adelaide had those.

Then Anne said what she had planned to say earlier.

"What I didn't tell you about was something else. Well, something that you might not have understood. What you first must know is that I really do love Aunt Addie. I'm not running from anything. I mean, I came here less with that in mind than in just settling down. She won me."

Anne twitched a little, her head falling less coyly, and she clicked her fingernails together.

"I've never talked about this," she said, "not even to Aunt Addie, who, of course, would understand. I'm actually flattered that you told me about yourself. You understand that?"

"OK."

"But there's something, too, that you don't understand about me. I don't know exactly how to explain that I really am a . . . well, it seems silly to put it this way . . . I really am a Christian. This place makes it difficult, you see. It's almost as if being part of Boldface Abbey was also taking a cynic's view of the things it's supposed to stand for. I'm not a cynic."

She tried to show the honesty in her statement by touching him. She put her hand on Owen's shoulder and smiled.

It wasn't the touch so much as it was the kindness which rang clear. He couldn't bear it that she really meant what she was saying. It was he who spoke in such platitudes; and he had never once remembered actually believing them. At

144

this moment, whatever had been those former urges to believe in what the church taught, indeed, in what monasticism demanded, could not have been more sour. And Anne Hone, far from being the comfort he wanted, seemed urgently to flaunt her contentment with those principles that he couldn't possibly endure. He felt disinterested and detached and lonely still, the very flesh in his insides feverish for the release he supposed had secretly been awaiting him from the moment he had decided to go to her house.

Anne's face was demure as she rested her hand, and he took it then quickly as though to pump from it the sustenance that he wanted. He leaned forward blankly and tried to kiss her.

She said, "I meant it when I said that I'm happy."

He pushed still further, too, resisting completely the idea that she was — he wanted to avoid the word — *good*. Yet the power that he possessed, and her continued attempt to stop this only when it was time, had served to crystallize his weakness. Owen tore at her dress. He felt compelled to destroy what tormented him with such complacency now. And Anne finally resisted as though it might wildly have tormented him further. He forced her to her feet, expecting to be aware of her smell. His body fit too; he told her that, and she asked him please to let her go. He let the anger grow in favor of what his confreres would think of him. He recalled the novice master's repeated statement that wearing the habit always kept one in touch with the office of the priesthood; it kept one from sin, he said, and Owen was happy to rip at the buttons extending the full length of his body. The cassock now seemed only to exacerbate the contempt he had for those who would have censured him. He held her well, after all. He didn't even think anymore of the silliness of the lines:

> Embrace me, you sweet embraceable you.
> Embrace me, you irreplaceable you.

Last of all, it wasn't just the release. For he felt urged to cry out at the air, felt his body itself, and then a need to have it run free as he supposed it should always have been. He breathed at Anne as he breathed out his confinements, not the mere pathway that had led him to this, but life itself: that existence whose breath *did* portend dependencies.

Her breasts yielded to him coarsely, and she fought even more stubbornly to save him. She told him that she did like him. "You are an attractive man. You *do* laugh, you *can* let go . . ."

Weren't there supposed to be quiet imaginings of tranquillity coming from her breath? The sound of water and the glare of light and winds coming at his face and moving about his ears and forehead?

He measured nothing, having let go the last imagining of his power. He thought the inevitable until Anne had simply gone limp in his arms. He looked at her with all the former impulses breaking, the machinery grinding.

She asked him if he was finished as she cried, telling him how difficult it had been once you realized that it takes a kind of decency to really believe. That, last, this must be the final horror to any man who suspects himself of his decency.

"At last you might believe me," she said. "Do you believe me now? *Do you believe me now!*" Her face wore condolences instead of censure. She looked at him wanting him to accuse her, not watching for him to hate her. She told

146

him that she was sorry that it didn't mean what he had wanted it to. But she wasn't laughing or offering any more consoling gestures. She limped past him still crying a little. She talked about it as if she were perfectly aware of his pain.

Anne said, "As for my remarks about love, there was somebody once in Spain. I'll spare you the romantic elements by saying that we'd loved each other for most of the time I was there. Until that time I'd felt like you. He was a teacher at Salamanca, where I went to school, you see. He was also married; he had children. His wife was kind, but I nearly destroyed her. I nearly destroyed myself. If you're interested, I found my way out with confession. If you'd really listened to me the past few years, you might have figured it out. I might even have needed you."

She went to her room then, and he hated her. He actually *hated* her and only the child in him had adequate defenses. He left, reveling in self-pity. He went to the chapel where he unleashed merely the energy of his disgust. He discovered no final words, and the final disbelief with which he also damned God was only the token of another awakening urge. But Father Brendan Price had already said that it was death Owen really worried about.

The silence in the old building framed him rigidly, and he was amazed that he heard no explosions. In the hallway the novices had rubbed down the floors with oil, the only thing they had found, over the years, capable of keeping down the dust. He was used to the smell.

Small patches of dirt and lint lay at the doors of priests who, according to custom, had swept the trash of their rooms there. The novices had dutifully attempted to clean these, but had left most of the dirt.

147

The reverie lasted through the passageways and built up again as he went to his room. He lay on the bed, sinking into the ancient mattress, and stared at the poster on the far wall: Gandhi. He thought of gurus and such, and of nirvana. Owen knew no one who had been there, though he had expected, when he first came to the monastery, to find it.

He laughed to think that Anne Hone actually had this.

He got up and undressed and turned on the reading lamp and stood before the mirror. His body seemed, as ever, manly enough, and he flexed his arms against the small light as though he might have been Adonis at last, in case the perfection that monks seek in the name of mankind as a whole should suddenly have been crystallized in his release. This he liked. He rubbed the hair of his chest in cosmic fulfillment, and he put his hands down further and all along was thinking toward the moment of release that he hadn't had with Anne. Then his realization of its passing, as she might have said, and the resumption of the former state of mind.

He wondered that the monks would now have spoken of the horror of it, and he thought that Abbot Giles knew now, and it would only be a matter of time.

TWENTY   ABBOT GILES had been up most of the night,
his mind not at all on Owen Cline and, for that matter, not at
all on one specific thing. But focus, at least, was on the speck
of ceiling paint which was now the largest and most notice-
able particle on his desk.

His journal lay open, the top page scrawled and crossed
out and unreadable.

A man must first judge himself was the thought that
comforted him, but he felt unsafe since it wasn't scriptural.
There was no use going to any canon or to spiritual writers,
but he had to have justification. He must explain what he
had done.

Moreover, the responsibility of his position suddenly
seemed to stare more steadily in his face. The former abbots
no longer haunted him about this; now it was God himself.
He didn't try to explain it and held his hands over his face
and rocked back and forth in the chair. How could he even
have enjoyed the celebration, let alone undertake to build a
new monastery?

He began to examine the past. He thought to make the battle only a momentary one and mumbled: oh men living together so long in one place, starving themselves of women. But he knew women, attractive ones, and he heard their confessions, he talked to them. He was startled to think that there hadn't been any other interest.

What, then, of his association with men?

He had already fought too much with the variety of strangers who populated his monastery. He didn't trust the manner by which they often seemed saints and other times a menagerie of broken souls. What of the saints now? What, say, of Father Lucas who, this moment, lay in the infirmary in the last stages of carcinoma? Any of them there, whose lives were perpetual agonies. They bore it well enough, and yet Father Lucas, their example, did so by drawing cemetery scenes with crayons.

Giles could think of no single confrere who bore his personal burdens with any sort of sanity.

This was where he fled now, daring to call his trouble a part of the human condition. Were they not all tinged with insanity then? Should he think now that what he learned about himself was his private stock of it?

What also, now, of Vinnie? Whose life was riddled with those undefined calamities? Giles was recalling Vinnie's presence and the pleasure. Something beyond the physical — peace. He thought also of Brendan Price and his Myrtis. The abbot touched his own face severely. His mind rested brightly on the idea of him and Vinnie, like Brendan and Myrtis, being up somewhere together where no one could touch them. Each knowing exactly the feelings of the other.

So he must call Vinnie.

He looked back to the pages of his journal which described his feelings. He dialed the number with conviction.
Ring, ring, ringring.

The nurse answered and got him and Vinnie told him right away:

"Well, I *am* seeing a patient right now . . ."

"Vinnie, it's terrible down here."

"I might have guessed that it would be, but, listen, don't . . ."

"We have to talk about it, don't we?"

"Yeah, yeah."

"A minute, Vinnie."

"I've got patients, I've . . ."

"Damn it, you sound as if you're suddenly changing your . . ."

Vinnie had moved the receiver and Giles could hear talking, a door closing.

"Listen, Father, I really don't know what caused that. I don't know why I did it and . . ."

The hedging terrified Giles. He didn't want to hear it. He *couldn't* hear it.

"Vin, you're not going to put it down; you're *not* going to renege. God, you're not."

"I was depressed."

"Not Sunday morning, Vinnie! God, not Sunday."

"You can read whatever you want. I just have to tell you that I'm not that way."

"Damn it, *what* way?"

"Well, I'm not . . . It would be futile, Father. What about your job, what about . . ."

"Vin . . . I . . ."

"In fact, I was going to tell you that I think we ought to get some distance from each other. I was going to tell you that I've finally decided to close down practice. I need to get away. I *have* to go, or, well . . . it's me, and time I learned to live with myself. I can't explain it . . ."

"Vinnie . . ."

"Because when I try to define it, the whole thing disappears and I'm sick of it."

"Vinnie, the human condition is . . ."

"To hell with the human condition. I mean, that disappears with your kind of distinctions too. Go back to your monks."

"Listen to me, Vinnie, now just listen a minute: I want to talk about it. I'll come down there. Give me two hours . . ."

"I really have to go now. My patients."

"What about all the past? What about . . . all the things I've done for you? What about the things you owe me?"

"I'm going to hang up now."

"Vinnie, look!"

"I owe you more than I'll ever be able to pay back. This just isn't the way to do it."

"Vinnie, I'll die here."

"There's no one holding you."

"God, Vin, I don't believe you're talking to me this way."

"Listen, I do have to go. I'll be in touch some time. It's going to take a long time, I think."

Giles was frightened by his sudden anger. His mind went wildly through all the things he might have said, and he held the phone as though it were a last contact with reality.

He sat dazed, then, retracing all the moments, tried to fathom how he must have misread them. He couldn't dismiss that awareness which spoke of Vinnie's full cooperation. Had he not, in fact, urged on the subtler moments too; hadn't he been the most practiced and the most vulnerable? He recalled only one thing. Vinnie said, "I'm resisting the temptation to run from this," and Giles felt the hesitation. That was what he could remember now as though it were a lifetime sentence.

He squirmed in the chair until he had fixed his eyes on the ceiling. He went to the window and looked toward the water tank, finally attaching a significance to the position of the sun. It was like a host over a chalice, and then he held up an imaginary chalice; he put the host above it, remembering suddenly the old Latin formula: *Corpus Domini Nostri Jesu Christi custodiat animam tuam in vitam aeternam.*

The Amen rang loudly, and he trusted it suddenly as if it had recaptured a lost vision. He imagined himself giving out communion, and the rapt faces of the faithful, their corporate anticipation. He saw the old women at Good Friday services, crawling the last few feet of the way to kiss the crucifix. There were children parading with assumed dignity at being brought to the altar for the first time. It was a splendid picture of mankind raised above its momentary worries. Abbot Giles felt soiled beside this picture, and he let his hands down slowly. The world of his thought was of ordered moments.

He stiffened. He took out the plans for the new monastery and coldly fixed his signature of approval to each sheet. He had in mind again the meetings with architects and bankers. He got out the Boldface seal, his own crest. He must have a new one. He fashioned a new coat of arms, a

153

physician's seal, a host and chalice, a figure representing light.

He selected a fresh sheet of paper from inside his stack of official stationery.

He wrote frantically:

FROM THE OFFICE OF THE ABBOT CONCERNING COMPLAINING AND THE WORLD: NEW MEASURES

In the interests of restoring an order which will, in the future, secure a community not apt to stray to follies and material concerns, the following decrees are made:
1) No monk of Boldface Abbey will own, procure, or accept anything from anybody anywhere
2) Monks will not moan and complain about things they don't have and needn't have
3) Sense will be guarded, henceforth, against pleasures which don't befit the conduct of monks
4) No monk will have electric fans; no monk will have inordinate friendships

Other measures will be forthcoming.

† Giles, abbot

He posted that on the bulletin board outside the door and for two days he fasted and prayed. He tried not to think of Vincent Dano, and he stayed inside where they couldn't find him.

TWENTY-ONE   CONTROVERSY BROKE to the rafters, of
course, and they swore all together that he had at last lost his
mind and was returning them to the dark ages. When they
knocked at the door often and he sent them away, they held
meetings.

The factions emerged as most would have expected, the
old against the young, the psychologists against the theologians, the traditionalists against the moderns.

"I will leave," a young monk said.

"Do so," replied Affirmo Biggsbee, and in the midst of it
certain of them did pack bags. It was a world lubricated with
the full monastic concern and they didn't worry about survival. Owen Cline alone was the one who stood by in-
differently.

He laughed to see them goading each other into specula-
tion. He listened to find both argument and solution crum-
bling against the abbot's continued refusal to appear. He
went to the door himself and asked to have a word, and it was
to him that Giles finally offered the last phase of his plan.

Through the door he told Owen to get the monks together, and he posted a Saturday morning time for the chapter meeting at which he would explain everything. Owen likewise watched the old buildings buzz with the activity of those who would argue their case from canon law; those who would site expertly the decrees from the Second Vatican Council; those with arguments from psychology; those from anthropology, this vast microcosm of all reality.

These were the more precise factions, he thought:

The Old and Inaccessible
Father Olaf Dotis, novice master and censor librorum
Father Leo Dean, infirmarian and refectorian
Father Dismas Comstock, cellarer and typing teacher
Father Columban Sauer, professor of moral theology, assistant professor of philosophy, instructor in the clarinet
Father Cyril Drewe, teacher emeritus of ascetic theology
Father Affirmo Biggsbee, archivist, historian, professor of memorabilia
Abbot Wilfrid Coogan, resident movie-maker, deposed abbot

The Middle-of-the-Road
Father Phineas Rapp, professor of music, organist of Boldface Abbey chapel
Father Dunstan Gass, sub-prior, director of maintenance, professor of heating and plumbing
Father Willibald Gunther, professor of Romance languages and gardening
Father Robert Ewald, professor of popular culture, third-rate poet in residence
Father Lucas Dodd, portrait painter

Mild Detractors
Father Joachim McErlean, junior cleric, theologian
Father Thomas Gifford, electrician
Father Sanchez Jola, professor of Esperanza

Father Terence Hillis, instructor in weight-lifting
Father Eugene Klemperer, professor of movement
Father McDuff Moriarty, assistant dean of academic affairs

Utter Detractors
Father Alphonse Sloan, young theologian, practitioner of the
    Theory of Dichotomosis
Father Abel Coon, teacher of homiletics
Father Blaise Singleton, chaplain
Father Justice Bale, canonist
Father Gregorio Counihan, director of outer affairs

The Totally Oblivious
Father Owen Cline, instructor in the indefinite

Others undecided or sick
novices, lay brothers, domestics
38 monks, all told

The meeting:

It was somehow majestic that the room was extraordinarily well-lighted and the paintings of former abbots were standing guard like presidents in school classrooms.

Abbot Giles wore full regalia; he was clear-headed and imposing and the whisperers waited for twitches of the face, or foreign-sounding curses; for the sudden address to a table or a wall. But almost all had seen that he possessed a new, unsubtle identity that made both the garb and the demeanor fitting.

It was the curious reverence which they recognized for the authority which was represented. And the inevitable question was resolved by the historic answer: it was the nobility of one put into lordly circumstances; one didn't wrong such men in seeing flaws, but there was something almost indecent in attacking them. It had been this way with the deposing of Abbot Wilfrid. The old man had sat quietly and took even the most flagrant abuse — there was even an admirable humility as though he had been trained for it — and when they insisted en masse that he resign, he stood up quickly to do so. They quite forgot what they despised him for until the distance once again had separated the man from his office.

No one talked seriously of deposing Abbot Giles. It was, after all, only two years since he had taken office, and Rome would take a dim view of anything that hasty. When it came to it, there was also uncertainty as to what they ought to concentrate on.

First, they prayed. The abbot did it in an untimid voice, calling on the Virgin. She was his symbol of purity, though he steeled his feelings against reproach. This was duty.

For the most part he took his strength from specters of other times he had seen. He did not flinch in this determination. When the prayer was done, he said, "I know you and I know what you are thinking and I know that there is no way to deal with it."

"If I may say so," someone boomed immediately, "your behavior the past few days has been . . . well, peculiar."

"I have been praying. *That* is not peculiar."

"In the dark, behind the door, inaccessible. Your decrees are antediluvian."

"Is that it?" the Abbot asked. It was a matter of their having got quickly to the point so that now he could say everything. "This discipline is timely," he said. "Monks aren't supposed to be worldlings."

"But we are products of our time."

"With duties to our vows."

"Yes and we must show a falling world the values of Christian witness."

"What is Christian witness? That's the point."

"And the revival of faith in a faithless world."

"Of God's forgiveness."

"Of God's justice."

"God's mercy."

"God's living concern for mankind."

It was Father Affirmo's turn. He stared at the abbot with continuing aversion. But his interest was piqued. The cigarettes, as usual, flamed out frequently.

"Ultimately our lives need no defense," he said. "Look at us; we are not together here with guns, and we haven't come to kill."

They were, in general, amazed. They reflected, trying to make the gathering friendlier.

"It's the same question; what are we really arguing about?"

The abbot said, "We are not arguing. I have made the rules, and when the new monastery is built you will see that . . ."

"Abbot, you can't really mean this?" Phineas said.

"We shall survive," the abbot said.

Another said, "That is ridiculous."

"Am I your abbot or not?"

"That is not the question," Father Phineas said. "The question is something else altogether."

It began with the premise of an abbot's rights, which from antiquity were held to be absolute. The abbot held the place of Christ, the Holy Rule said, and for this it had prescribed absolute obedience. There were allowances for irregular abbots, to be sure, those which gave him the authority to order them as he pleased, for instance; but reforms had supposed that absentee abbots were a thing of the past. The Rule also allowed that a monk was free to disagree and show that disagreement: Statute 33, Section One: *if a monk finds that he cannot in conscience do what his abbot orders, he will first offer his reason humbly to the abbot; if the monk cannot be persuaded of his error, he will, in humility, accede to the abbot's decree, even should it involve personal discomfort.*

Here Giles had them. He quoted the statute and they questioned the matter of conscience and he stood with firmer determination and he said, "Yes, but the fact remains. I see it this way, and I am the abbot."

He was not hesitating, though for the moment he had not steeled himself against a recollection of Vinnie. Vinnie was still there, somehow, pushing at him. Giles had himself in mind more than he had them in mind. But he had substituted his weakness for theirs, not in accord with his own crime. In accord with the condition of man, rather; not Giles Logan, but weakness; not monks, but weariness. He fought lest he break, and the vivid possibility of his office coming to nothing, of his monastery amounting to nothing, sustained him.

He had read them the OPERATING SUGGESTIONS as a final evidence that they were, indeed, too caught by the allurements of the world. He stared aggressively at each, and especially at Father Owen, who, in his mind, seemed another shape of his own weakness. So were they all, then, if the truth were known. He thought of Brendan Price and the pathetic side of him which might finally have brought him despair. This couldn't be Christian.

160

He watched the puzzled faces. That vision of himself as *abbas,* Father, suddenly clicked beyond any image he had ever given himself. This had come forth from his own measure of disillusionment. Each day of his isolation he had promised himself that he wouldn't fail, and that, above all, he would be articulate. The dismal truth was that he hadn't been articulate enough. Need he really convince them with words? For this he assured himself that propriety should never have been put down at his door. He would explain and confess his own sins if he had to.

But this was carrying it too far. Giles's face, he imagined, must have reddened in the moment of awakening, and he felt himself slowly going backward. At last the lights came and he didn't discount them.

"I am your abbot. You elected me and my rules stand as I have stated them!"

His eyes fell immediately; he mumbled to himself, and gathered the OPERATING SUGGESTIONS, and then scattered them.

"Well, damn it. Well. We are going to have discipline. You are going to work, I mean *work;* and we are going to pray."

He fell down calling loudly to God. He asked them to pray with him, beginning from memory to recite Psalm 42: "Do me justice, O God, and fight my fight against a faithless people; from the deceitful and impious man rescue me. For you, O God, are my strength . . ."

More than half the assembly had joined him. Seeing him pray had stilled them; had given them that comfort that most had come to the monastery for; that comfort of acknowledging their weaknesses, perhaps, but more so of being able to do so in the company of other men. Each had found

161

it, as such, both the consolation it had been formerly, and a rescue from whatever it was that no one of them had been able to see in their meeting. No, it wasn't an insane act, or a deluded abbot leading them into oblivion; it was, finally, a full statement of a dependency that no individual lately acknowledged outside his own cell. It was *there*, dark to the world and secretly, that most became desperate and coddled their fragile humanity. There they could have done this, but now it was different.

The chatter of those who had not agreed, of those who had seen only the excess of formula and its delusion, cautiously sought the shelter of shrugs and limp nods. They had tried to speak, and, not being heard, they settled in momentary bewilderment, leaving with sharp-tongued whispers, taking to their rooms with private sermons, writing out their protests, searching the books of the law.

It was finally over and few left without the feeling of at least an ambiguous uplift. This stirred on and on. It was a revival.

Boldface Abbey was silent, and, in the main, the afternoon saw few words spoken except for the soft drone of the refectorian's voice ordering the kitchen help in their duties. The nearby traffic buzzed as usual, set with the heat and warmly surrounding the ancient buildings of the Institute campus. No one walked the avenue, and the shutters were drawn. The long corridors were uninhabited but for the reckless sun which broke solemnly through the opaque glass of windows on the south side where no shutters were. The aged ferns lining these hallways bent cautiously against the burden of surviving only on the sunlight, the dead ones grown into straw and lining moldings where the novices

162

hadn't swept. The novices had been at Spiritual Reading, the abbot's rule.

The night arrived out of this with a meal taken in silence, and, after Office, the monks had retired with notable allegiance to the revival spirit.

TWENTY-TWO   FATHER OWEN, absorbed by the silence, now tried sleep as if it were the final spasm of a drawn-out illness. He wasn't surprised that he found sleep difficult. Nor was he surprised at last to be indifferent about the day's events.

He wasn't resisting the emerging cold view of his monastery's history, which, now especially, seemed riddled with Giles Logan's sort of mania. Whoever would have believed, to begin with, that a Romish monastery could survive in the north Georgia Bible belt, but for the emotional stamina of Alcuin Hegel who arrived on a winter morning in 1900 and stretched out his arm and claimed it all for the Lord? It was perhaps his madness alone, like Giles's, that had dreamed Boldface Abbey into existence. The leadership, facts indicated, was little more than the weight of authority the church places with any hierarch and the intimidations which defiance of that authority generated. The old man, apparently, had stood up from time to time and harangued them into acceptance of whatever method was expedient for their survival. This was the Christian in him. It was Anne Hone's Christianity that they might have gone whole winters with little food because Alcuin Hegel had made them scale it to exact portions. Now might not Giles Logan merely be exercising those ritual forms which had in the past brought the abbey through crises?

Whatever the answer to this, Owen was certain that he no longer cared. The darkened room continued to breathe on him the specters of his once full assent to its modes of operation, its rules, its eccentricities.

His mind went to Anne, *her* words, *her* indulgence.

Here he was clearly tormented, but felt a growing peace as if her indictment had in some way pinpointed a discontent that had been too carefully hidden from him. How purposeful it seemed that the blind spots in the machinery of existence were so simply geared.

He couldn't call her, and he supposed that he would never live it down. He couldn't ever go back there; he couldn't be forgiven. He wondered that she hadn't called the police. And that thought seemed a further reason for hating her. But then he started allowing himself a richer view of his own motives in the matter. Ha, it was, after all, a premise that *he* had invented or intensified out of very little. Anne was right that the problem was his.

What, then, that it went on with so few possible definitions? Owen Cline, God's rapist.

He wanted it to be over, and he lay in the bed slowly taking his clothes off as if to find the awarenesses which Anne described. He had wished this before as well; never coming to it without distraction; never quite sinking totally to that bottom point at which the earth beneath him was permitted its proper function. To hold him up, to force him to feel the solid mass underneath his shoulders. This, he imagined, must be at least the token of what it meant to recognize a basic outcry.

He was crying again.

He didn't worry about being a child now, or about following all the urges he was accustomed to with complete attention. He *was* aware of himself in accordance with what Anne Hone had taught him. He had skipped supper to avoid having the moment interfered with by usual overeating. Presently he was consumed with the feeling, for instance, of the elastic of his drawers as he slid them off, and he lay with his legs spread so that he also felt the air.

He took pleasure then in getting up, walking the hallway outside, down to the linen closet at its end, naked, getting clean sheets. He walked back to his cell slowly, hoping that someone would see. That pleasure wasn't explainable, either, but he thought of St. Francis throwing himself naked into the arms of the bishop, of Christ disrobing to wash his apostles' feet. He strutted with the cynicism; he held the clean cold sheets next to himself and enjoyed their smell.

He changed them slowly, drawing the folds naturally against himself as the sheets fell to the bed. He held in his belly.

He went back into the hallway, down to the shower, a cavernous room that had once been the fourth floor commissary. The shower had six heads; he turned them all on, felt the water from each, put them each on with a different pressure. He danced there, careful to be aware of the flowing water. In flux, it poured over his eyes like light.

In his cell again Owen locked the door as usual, opened the windows wide, and looked down on the darkened garden below. At this hour the silence was particularly sober. He could hear customary sounds, occasional automobiles passing on the perimeter road. He leaned forward out the window, felt the evening air. He rubbed his shoulder in it, the shower water drying by this power.

Then back to the bed where he lay holding the sides of his legs like electric clamps. He felt the warmth in his hands there. And he moved, thereafter, on the bed, into each of its large corners, loving the coolness.

He already had a clean handkerchief which he rubbed about himself. He imagined that his body might have been an athlete's and how he loved thinking it strong and Grecian. He had always wanted this, too, formerly ashamed even to think of what he might have looked like, say, in a pair of wrestling trunks. Owen Cline, God's Adonis. The drawers he got in the commissary were dismally ordinary; he laughed to think that he might have agreed with Father Affirmo's thought that they needed a better variety of underwear.

At any rate, the thought of having only the covering of his drawers alone stimulated him. He took the handkerchief and draped it around himself. He fitted it under himself then.

He had his wrestling trunks when he had tied two hand-kerchiefs together. The variety startled him.

He *was* aware of everything in himself. He imagined the fresh cells winding about his thoughts, his mind going like a great factory; yet an immense smoothness. Anne was finally there as well and the thought of embarrassing moments which were always too embarrassing. She hadn't really touched

167

him. She had looked at him as he had wanted, her own body in careful motion, each of them, as he wished, aware, aware.

Somehow, too, there was no embarrassment in his thinking of himself content. He might have been St. Francis again. Owen's repentance lay somewhere in this extreme, its freedom, then its urges.

For that, at last, he had to be the Christian that Anne had talked about too; and free, he had to ascend whatever the pinnacle of this moment's release incautiously. It was high in the air, coming from the windows as though from the distant past. His hands moved slowly while he felt the sudden, perfectly apt cruelty governing the movement.

So that Owen Cline, God's body, danced to this strange music and to the darkness. He went about the room as though he were a part of it, leaning against the walls, touching himself to the walls, the door, the furniture. Then, last of all, the window where he climbed with slow plodding determination. He was determined as well that the air should deliver him as everything else did.

He stood in the window against this air, believing himself finally a part of it too. He flung his hands up into the rafters of these old high ledges whose panes too benevolently reflected his motives; if the madness were madness, it was Christian madness!

And so, there, Anne!

Before he slipped and fell, as he partly might have wished, he reflected that he hadn't seen the new monastery that would have been the token of his new awareness. It was just as Brendan Price hadn't. Neither had he known those saints whose hearts he fancied were somehow truer than he could ever have been in repentance. No professional cross-bearer, he. No man.

And the child he considered himself had its mind locked into the last of Brendan's words to him. "It's death you're afraid of." And it was this that Owen had in mind when he felt himself gliding and swiftly panicking in the illusion that washed upon his body. He said that he couldn't be what Father Brendan was.

TWENTY-THREE   THERE WAS NO WAITING to have
the ground broken for the new monastery. Abbot Giles had
circulated word that he would do the ceremony after Lauds
next day. It had to be the only proper next move, seeing that
now he had them and had them the way an abbot must.
Even before breakfast they had gathered on the north side of
the property where a hasty straw vote had said the new building should go. Expediency prevailed, then, as Affirmo
quickly dressed the abbot in the best of Alcuin Hegel's copes,
the one he had always kept from Giles's hands.

But there was Giles, Affirmo by his side like a lieutenant,
the monks gathered around their new leader. They looked
contented and were off to do what must be done.

Abbot Giles loved the light, standing once again at the
head of the procession. He had also been careful to get word
to Miss Adelaide, thinking Owen Cline to have been the
right person to fetch her. With Owen absent, Giles had sent
Affirmo. And so there was the titmouse arriving, with the
monks waiting for her, and gracious. It was all a part of the

survival that she walked the entire distance with Anne, who now supported her aunt's arms as though it were the oldest comfort possible. Both, indeed, said that they knew their monks, all right.

Miss Hone said that she was glad to be there. "And you see that not even leucoplakia has kept *me* away; not the hour. This can mean only the most special things. You don't know what God and I know; I'm not telling."

They laughed at her self-deprecating gestures as Anne arranged her shawl for her against the slight morning chill.

And Giles's eyes responded with special haste, as was his custom now. In his eyes was couched perceptible energy, as if he were being also refreshed by private revelation. He was unable to think of anything but his lights, holding his hands forward in a giving gesture. This was for Vincent Dano.

But then it was a matter of his being led to preach to them of fortitude and the church's ancient mission to be in the thick of things; his own fear was of too much conviction. He waved his hands upward blithely, in submission to what he imagined in his own heart to be God's cancellation of a collective debt, Miss Adelaide its executor. Now he tried to think little of himself, but of the corporate person which was his monastery and his charge. *She* had taught him this strangely, and he held what he believed were *her* plans under his arm. He had his journal to represent himself. And he smiled against the ever-growing tears which confirmed that it wasn't the time to moan the tides of fortune or question God's plan. With a wild remoteness, he pulled his cassock around him tightly to take the first step.

The procession went past the south side of the monastery building and around the corner where the fourth-floor cells were. Giles blessed what he saw with particular attention. He was finally thinking that Boldface Abbey belonged to that age in which the real nature of humanity *could* be defined. Something in both his delayed sense of what was happening, and that remembrance of so many words having escaped him, turned his mind often to revelation. What he had accomplished in the resignation of his own will had been, he presumed, a kind of honesty, now uncertain, now only partial. But he did know that he had made them think together. What then that he should have been beset by lights, by sudden awareness of particles in the air, had it not been to tell him that reality had to be itself?

This belonged to all of them.

Giles held his head high, believing that he could also be uncertain and not have to worry about it. He thought that what he had falsely measured was the end toward which the present anonymity led them. He forgot that God protected them. He forgot that they really did know little about each other except for these laughable externals. God knew the inside where they were aptly vulnerable, as Miss Hone had said. These monks represented a world which Giles finally acknowledged had little faith but had consummate polity. It was only the loneliness of his office that created the burdens of ruling men who had come to the end of the human search.

For this he hadn't needed to count heads or to think of them even as individuals. He remembered Father Brendan at this moment and numbered the taint in each of them — his own taint, to be sure, Affirmo's (he was even ready to appoint him to whatever place in the hierarchy he wanted), Miss Hone's, Owen Cline's.

Then he had noticed that Owen was absent. He didn't

remember the details of their latest conversation, pushing it aside like all the rest. The procession had finally reached the point at which they would have to see him lying there; would have to come upon him on the side of the property where the fourth-floor cells were.

And they did.

It was just before Boldface's land had taken a new dignity in the reverence that this procession restored. It was just before the final, significant step toward the perimeter, where all the history belonged, that Giles first saw him in his handkerchiefs, the soft fabric loose at the edges of his body.

They didn't know him. Could they laugh that it was another deranged soul come to vent his last breath of contempt where it would mean the most?

They didn't rush, and there were only whispers of pity going up like dazzling lights. It was left to Giles once again to hold fast the revival against time and against folly. It just mustn't die in the wake of this final test that God had sent.

So that Miss Hone, his seeming representative, was the first to rush there. Having learned her controls as everybody knew, knowing the control that clouded even her private image of herself, she was led to make the final shrug in the way she always made it. To a degree, her eyes sparkled before she started to cry. And the significant detail now escaping her lay in the soft, almost girlish instinct by which she felt suddenly stronger and more faithful to her training.

Anne Hone followed her. What they did was look at each other with the particular grace of those with faith. Anne was close to her, admitting to herself that she wasn't behaving fearlessly. She might have wanted to apologize, yet supposing still the accuracy of her judgment, and not crying with anything but the simple brutality of her own clear thinking, she saw that the air had its spirals and the thick gentle motion of sunlight.

She cried loudly. She cried with the sobriety of trust, and with that touch of intelligible humility that said he was better off.

Others came around and took their decided views of the situation. They looked away, and the point is that they were thus further disposed to accept and live well by what Giles had to say about it. Quite solemnly and pontifically he lowered his own head in the emergent message: "We didn't know him. We think we know each other, but we don't."

But it suddenly hit him that Owen Cline had told him all of it; he measured it fully against his own needs as though God were still revealing. This sparkled on the high road of his dreams, like those moments when he told Vinnie what he really believed. The notebook which he dropped was a token of the fading significance. The sound of his heart was loud and he covered it with his hand. The distinction being made, he had caused the problem to disappear.

Miss Hone used her favorite word.

Anne Hone shored up her bosom.

Affirmo was the one who suddenly wept more loudly than the others, though he was again reduced to the fringes of things.

He said, "Is this a travesty, or what is this?"

Giles picked up Owen himself, carried the small body which coldly reflected the light and its ancient conspiracies, as though the deformity which had always been there ought to be spoken of as part of the accident. For this, Giles thought he knew that his own energy was no longer in words.

He almost smiled with the new faith in this, its splendid Christianity. Holding the body aloft, he told them to go on with the ground-breaking.

"Father Affirmo is rightly appointed to the position of my vicar. It's a new position and he is now second in command and he will do a splendid job of it."

He went to call the Rescue Squad and the police and the ambulance and sat in his office with the shades all the way up. He thought of those moments with Vinnie, but, more, of having no hostility toward any of his monks. He leaned forward over the monastery plans, knowing how important they were.

In a way he was very pleased that the phone at Vinnie Dano's office and the phone at his house rang and rang and rang.

Abbot Giles then made a memo:

FROM THE OFFICE OF THE ABBOT
CONCERNING: events of the past month
Accept these apologies of mine.

He called in Affirmo and they had their chat about Owen Cline's burial, and then about the reorganization of Boldface.

Affirmo was smiling flamboyantly, alive with all the possibilities, while Giles leaned up on his chair and farted, sighed, asked the wise old monk's viewpoint as to whether, in the new monastery plans, there were enough toilets.